Man OF Fantasy

ROCHELLE
ALERS

NATIONAL BESTSELLING AUTHOR

Man OF *Fantasy*

ARABESQUE®

Recycling programs
for this product may
not exist in your area.

MAN OF FANTASY

ISBN-13: 978-0-373-83164-7

www.kimanipress.com

Printed in U.S.A.

The BEST MEN series

You met Tessa, Faith and Simone—the Whitfields of New York and owners of Signature Bridals—in the WHITFIELD BRIDES series. Now meet three lifelong friends who fulfill their boyhood dream and purchase a Harlem brownstone for their business ventures.

Kyle Chatham, Duncan Gilmore and Ivan Campbell have worked tirelessly to overcome obstacles and achieve professional success, oftentimes at the expense of their personal lives. However, each will meet an extraordinary woman who just might make him reconsider what it means to be the best man.

In *Man of Fate,* high-profile attorney Kyle Chatham's classic sports car is rear-ended by Ava Warrick, a social worker who doesn't think much of lawyers and deeply mistrusts men. Ava expects the handsome attorney to sue her, not come to her rescue after she sustains a head injury in the accident. But Kyle knows he has to prove to Ava that he is nothing like the men in her past—a challenge he is prepared to take on *and* win.

Financial planner Duncan Gilmore's life is as predictable as the numbers on his spreadsheets. After losing his fiancée in the World Trade Center tragedy, he has finally begun dating again. In *Man of Fortune,* Duncan meets Tamara Wolcott—a beautiful and brilliant E.R. doctor with a bad attitude. As their relationship grows, Tamara begins to feel that she is just a replacement for his late fiancée. But Duncan knows that he has to put aside his pride if he's going to convince Tamara to be part of his life.

After the death of his identical twin years ago, psychotherapist Ivan Campbell is a "love 'em and leave 'em" guy who is afraid of commitment. But all of that changes in *Man of Fantasy* when he meets Nayo Goddard at an art gallery, where she is showing her collection of black-and-white photographs. Not only has she gotten Ivan to open up his heart to love again, she is also seeing another man. Ivan knows that he must prove that he is the best man for her, or risk losing her forever.

Yours in romance,

Rochelle Alers

Counsel is mine, and sound wisdom:
I am understanding; I have strength.
—*Proverbs* 8:14

Chapter 1

Ivan Campbell barely heard what the woman, who he'd been working closely with for the past two years renovating his Mount Morris brownstone, was rambling on about.

"Ivan, you're not listening to me."

He affected a half smile. "Yes, I am. You said *Architectural Digest* wants to do a layout of my place for an issue featuring New York City homes and apartments."

Carla Harris stared at the man with the sensual, brooding expression, wishing he would smile, because whenever Dr. Ivan Campbell did smile, it reminded her of pinpoints of sunlight breaking through dark storm clouds. She'd thought she was attracted to a certain type until she found herself face-to-face with the brilliant psychotherapist.

An inch shy of the six-foot mark, he could not disguise the perfection of his toned body, whether in a tailored suit or in casual attire. She didn't know why, but Carla preferred seeing Ivan casually dressed, as he was now, in a pair of jeans, short-sleeved shirt and running shoes. His aftershave was the perfect complement to his body's natural masculine scent.

"Okay, I apologize."

What passed for a smile quickly vanished as Ivan stared at Carla. They were sitting on soft leather chairs in a pale butter-yellow in an alcove off the living room designed for small, intimate gatherings—a room his mother had referred to as a parlor. He'd lit a fire in the fireplace to ward off an early-autumn chill. The fireplace was an architecturally minimalist design that resembled a hole set inside a low, horizontal box along a wide expanse of wall, without a mantel or surround. Large pillars in bronze candleholders of various heights and sizes were positioned off to one side of the stone hearth, accentuating the modern interior of the brownstone, which was situated in one of Harlem's most prominent historic districts.

Ivan knew Carla was flirting with him and had been since their initial meeting, which now seemed ages ago. He'd communicated, albeit subtly, that he didn't believe in mixing business with pleasure. His deep-set, intense, dark brown eyes met and fused with a pair of gray ones behind a pair of oversize horn-rims. The fire-engine-red glasses and flaming-red spiked hairdo had become Carla's signature look—a look that was a bit too funky for his tastes. Laid-back by nature, Ivan preferred women who were less flamboyant, whose manner of dress didn't call attention to themselves.

Carla took another sip from a bottle of sparkling water. "I know how much you value your privacy, Ivan, but I'll make certain your name and address don't appear anywhere in the piece."

Ivan knew what the layout would do for her career. It would be the first time Carla Harris's decorating skills would be displayed in the preeminent magazine of interior design. She was young, having just celebrated her twenty-eighth birthday, and she was not only ambitious, but aggressive. When she'd contacted him for an initial consultation, Carla refused to take no for an answer. She called him relentlessly every other day for three weeks until he'd finally relented, then worked closely with the architect to reconfigure spaces that would restore the century-old structure to its former grandeur.

"Thanks, Carla."

The designer pressed her vermilion-colored lips together until they resembled a slash of red across her pale face. "You don't have to sound so enthusiastic, Dr. Campbell."

"I know how much this means to you," Ivan said in

the comforting tone he always used with his patients, "and because it does, I'm going to agree to the magazine spread."

The interior designer's smile was dazzling. "Thank you, Ivan."

He inclined his head. "You're welcome, Carla."

Ivan wanted to tell her he couldn't care less about someone taking pictures of his residence. At the end of the day all he wanted was to come home and relax after spending hours with his patients and lecturing students as an adjunct college professor.

He'd purchased the abandoned, dilapidated brownstone more than three years ago. It took a year and a half to complete the renovations and another year to decorate the interior. He'd lost count of the number of hours he'd sat with Carla going over catalogs filled with tables, chairs, lamps, rugs, beds and kitchen appliances. Four stories and fifty-seven hundred square feet of living space that comprised a terrace, garden and patio, powered by solar panels and an organic garden, provided the perfect environment for living and entertaining.

The street-level space had a home theater, kitchen, bath, home office and gym. The second floor had a master bedroom, adjoining bath and two guest rooms with en suite baths. The brownstone contained two two-bedroom apartments on the third floor. One apartment he'd recently rented to young married professionals expecting their first child, and a real estate agent was setting up an interview with a recently married New York City couple currently living with their in-laws on Long Island.

Ivan still hadn't decided what he wanted to do with the fourth floor. The entire space was without interior walls, and he'd had the contractor put in a half bath and a utility kitchen. Not only did he own the brownstone, he was also one-third partner in another brownstone a short distance away that he and childhood friends Kyle Chatham and Duncan Gilmore used for business.

"The photo shoot will take place some time in early December, but I can't set a date until you do something for me," Carla said, interrupting his thoughts.

"What's that?"

"You are going to have to do something with the walls."

A slight frown appeared. "What's wrong with the walls?"

It'd taken him weeks to decide on the colors he wanted to paint the rooms. At first he'd decided to have the primer covered with shades of eggshell or oyster-white, then changed his mind because it was too sterile a palette.

"You need pictures, Ivan. The walls are naked, unfinished. It's like a woman going to a formal affair. She's wearing an evening gown, dress shoes, makeup and hairstyle but has neglected to put on any accessories. In other words, where are the earrings, necklace, ring or bracelet? She's beautiful, but incomplete."

"But I'm not into art."

Carla pressed her lips together again. "They don't have to be paintings."

"What else do people hang on their walls?"

"Sculpture," she suggested.

"I told you that I'm not into art."

"What about photography?" Carla argued softly.

"What about it?"

"Would you be opposed to framed and matted photos?"

The seconds ticked off as Ivan thought about the designer's suggestion. He did have a framed photograph of Malcolm X in his home office that had been taken by his father, who'd attended a Harlem rally in 1964 to hear the charismatic Muslim leader speak. In 1999 the U.S. Postal Service issued a stamp of Malcolm X and Ivan had bought the framed stamp, placing it alongside the photo taken by the elder Campbell.

"No."

Carla exhaled deeply as she reached for her tote, searched through it and handed Ivan an envelope. "This is an invitation to an opening at a gallery featuring an exquisite collection of black-and-white photographs."

Ivan removed the printed card from the envelope. The invitation was for later that evening. "Are you going?" he asked Carla.

"No. I attended a preview a couple of days ago. They are magnificent, Ivan."

"Why didn't you pick up a few photographs for me?"

Carla saw the sensual smile and heard laughter in Ivan's query. "I would have, but art is very personal. I know what colors and fabrics you prefer, yet I have no idea what you'd like hanging on your walls."

Ivan sobered again. He knew the designer was right. He never tired of looking at photographs of Malcolm X.

"Okay, I'll go. But if I don't find anything I like, then you're going to have to improvise."

"Improvise how, Ivan?"

"Rent whatever you feel would complement the rooms and decor, and return them after the photo shoot."

He knew his reluctance to put any art on the walls was rooted in a childhood aversion to seeing clothes hanging from hooks or large nails in tarpaper shacks. As a boy, he and his identical twin were sent down South to visit their grandparents. At least, that was what his parents said, but Ivan knew the real reason was to keep them off Harlem's streets where they might possibly get into trouble. He'd befriended another boy whose parents were sharecroppers, and the first time he visited their house Ivan was stunned to find there were no doors or closets. Rooms were separated by curtains, and clothes were hung on hooks or large nails affixed to walls. The odor from whatever his friend's mother cooked clung to his clothes, and Ivan had recurring dreams of chickens, pigs and fish coming out of the walls to attack him.

Carla clasped her cavernous tote. She picked up a black angora shawl and wrapped it around her shoulders. "That sounds like a plan." She stood up. "Now that we've settled that I'll be on my way. I'll call you on Monday to find out if you found anything to your liking."

Ivan escorted Carla to the front door, hugged her and then watched as she walked to where she'd parked her red Mini Cooper. He closed the oak door with its leaded-glass pane after she'd maneuvered away from the curb.

Retracing his steps, he returned to the alcove, sitting and staring at the dying embers. Fall was his least favorite season of the year. It wasn't just the cooler temperatures, shorter days, longer nights and falling leaves, but rather, the reminder of the time he'd lost his twin brother in a senseless drive-by shooting.

Ivan had thought twenty-five years was more than enough time to accept that Jared was gone and was never coming back. But whenever the season changed, it reminded him of holding his dying brother in his arms while autumn leaves rained down on the cold ground while they waited for an ambulance.

He'd wanted to spend his day off doing absolutely nothing, but the call from Carla had altered his plans. At first he thought of telling her he had papers to grade, which he did. But when he'd heard the excitement in her voice, Ivan remembered his promise to the designer that he would do everything he could to help her business. And that meant opening his home to strangers who wanted to photograph the interior.

Leaning to his right, he picked up the invitation. Getting out and attending the showing was what he needed, not obsessing about the loss of his brother. Yes, he mused, he would get out of the house, go to the opening and hopefully find something he could hang on his walls. He scrolled through his cell-phone contacts and punched in the number for a car service, telling the dispatcher he needed a car within the hour.

He owned a classic 1963 Chevrolet Corvette Stingray, which he stored in a nearby garage, but he'd decided not to drive downtown, where there was little or no parking, and risk having his car towed.

Forty-five minutes later, showered and shaved, he closed the door to his brownstone and walked over to the Town Car parked across the tree-lined street. The driver, leaning against the bumper, straightened and opened the rear door.

"Thank you, Robert," Ivan said, smiling as he ducked his head to get into the vehicle. The dispatcher knew he liked riding with the elderly chauffeur.

"You're welcome, Dr. Campbell."

Ivan gave the driver the address of the gallery in Greenwich Village, then settled back to relax and enjoy the ride downtown.

His smile faded with the slam of the solid door.

People in the neighborhood had begun calling him Dr. Campbell, rather than Ivan or Mr. Campbell. Referring to him by his title was not only too formal, but pretentious. There was one thing he knew he wasn't, and that was pretentious.

He'd decided to become a psychologist, not to help people deal with their psychological or emotional problems, but to find out who Ivan Garner Campbell actually was, how to come to grips with his childhood. It'd taken years, but he'd accepted the advice he gave his patients: "Take control of your fears before they stop you from living your good life."

He'd set up a private practice, purchased a brownstone in the Harlem historic district and dated women who kept his interest for more than a few hours—all that attributed to him living his good life.

Nayo Goddard felt as if she'd been holding her breath since Geoffrey Magnus opened the doors of the gallery for the caterer and his staff to set up for the opening of her extensive collection of black-and-white photographs. She found herself humming along to the prerecorded music of a string quartet.

The curious and critics from the art world sipped champagne, nibbled on caviar on toast points, sushi and tiny finger sandwiches while peering intently at the matted photos displayed around the expansive space in the beautiful, 1850s Italianate row house. The SOLD stickers affixed to three-quarters of the photographs exhibited was an indication that her first showing was a rousing success.

"You did it, darling."

Shifting slightly, Nayo smiled up at her patron and best friend. "It looks as if we did it," she said softly.

Her dark brown eyes met and fused with a large, soft, dove-gray pair. Geoffrey Magnus had encouraged her to follow her dream of becoming a photographer, even though her parents believed she'd wasted her time and education indulging in a frivolous hobby. Tall and slender with a mop of curly blond hair, Geoff was a trust-fund baby and the grandson of one of the most prominent art dealers and collectors in the Northeast.

His grandparents, who'd honeymooned in Mexico, met Frida Kahlo and her muralist husband, Diego Rivera, and purchased Frida's *Self-Portrait with Monkey.* Their love affair with Mexican art fueled a passion that continued throughout their lifetime. Besides Mexican art, Geoff's parents preferred folk art and spent most of their time traveling throughout the U.S. and the Caribbean looking for new talent. The result was one of the most extensive collections of nine-teenth- and twentieth-century North and South American art ever assembled. Geoff followed in the family tradition when he enrolled at Pratt Institute and earned a degree in the history of art and design.

Nayo's grandmother had surprised her with a graduation gift of an all-expense-paid trip to Europe for the summer. It was there she'd met Geoff when he was a student at Pratt in Venice, a six-week summer program in which students studied painting, art history, drawing, printmaking and Venetian art. She and Geoff hung out together for two weeks before Nayo traveled south to Rome. They'd exchanged telephone numbers, and it was another six months before they were reunited. Nine years later, Geoff and Nayo, thirty and thirty-one respectively, were still friends. She knew he wanted more than friendship, but she knew that becoming intimate would ruin their relationship. Her mantra "If it isn't broke, don't try to fix it" had served her well.

Geoff handed Nayo a flute of champagne, touching her glass with his. "Congratulations."

Taking a sip, she smiled at him over the rim. "Thank you."

Ivan moved slowly from one photograph to another, not wanting to believe he'd find himself so entranced with bridges. All the photos were numbered and a catalog identified the city and state in which the bridges were located. There were covered bridges in New England hamlets, beam-and-truss bridges in the Midwest and Pacific Northwest, natural-arch bridges in the Southwest and cable-stayed bridges along the East and West coasts.

The photographer, who went by the single name of Nayo, had captured the natural beauty of the landscapes regardless of the season. He'd found himself staring intently at a triptych of a snow-covered bridge in New Hampshire. The first shot was taken at sunrise, the second when the sun was at its zenith and the third at dusk. It was the same bridge, yet the background in each photo looked different because of the waning light and lengthening shadows.

Ivan uttered an expletive. He was too late. Someone had already purchased the trio of photographs. He tapped the arm of a passing waiter. "Excuse me. Can you please direct me to the photographer?"

The waiter pointed to a petite woman wearing a white, man-tailored blouse and black pencil skirt. "That's Miss Nayo."

Ivan smiled. "Thank you."

He stared at the young woman with skin the color of milk chocolate. Her short, curly hair was the perfect complement to her round face. Throwing her head back, she was laughing as she stood next to a tall, blond man. Ivan found himself as enthralled with the photographer as he was with her work. The diamond studs in her pierced ears caught the light. The wide belt around her narrow waist matched her black, patent-leather, peep-toe pumps.

Weaving his way through the throng that was eating, drinking and talking quietly, Ivan approached the photographer. "Miss Nayo?"

Nayo turned to stare at the man standing only a few

feet from where she stood with Geoff. Her practiced eye took in everything about him in one sweeping glance. He was tall and exquisitely proportioned. The jacket of his charcoal-gray suit, with its faint pinstripe, draped his shoulders as if it had been tailored expressly for him. A pale gray shirt with French cuffs and a silk tie in a flattering aubergine pulled his look together.

He was more conservatively dressed than the others who favored the ubiquitous New York City black. Her gaze moved slowly from his cropped hair and distinctive widow's peak to his lean mocha-brown face and masculine features.

Her lips parted in a warm smile. She extended her hand. "It's just Nayo."

"Ivan Campbell." He took her hand, and it disappeared into his much larger one. She'd pronounced her name Naw-yo.

Nayo felt a slight jolt at the contact, and she quickly extricated her fingers to cut off the electricity. "Mr. Campbell, how may I help you?" she asked as Geoff walked away. Whenever she interacted with a potential client, Geoff made it a practice not to ingratiate himself.

Ivan found himself transfixed by Nayo's face. Upon closer inspection, she looked as if she was barely out of high school. Her makeup was natural and flawless. The soft highlights on her eyelids complemented her lip gloss and the subtle blush on her high cheekbones. Her round eyes afforded her a slightly startled look. And it was through those eyes she was able to capture incredible images. When he'd stared at the photos of bridges, he felt as if he were viewing them through the camera lens.

"Carla Harris suggested I come to your showing to purchase some of your work. I need artwork for my walls for a magazine layout. I have no interest in paintings or sculpture, but I'm not opposed to photography."

Nayo smiled and an elusive dimple deepened in her left cheek. "Carla is an extremely talented designer."

"I agree," Ivan replied. "She's turned my home into quite the showplace."

"That's Carla. Have you seen anything you like?"

Yes, I have, Ivan thought. He wanted to tell Nayo she was as stunningly beautiful as her photographs. "Yes, I have but…" His words trailed off when her smile grew wider.

Nayo's eyebrows lifted. "What is it, Mr. Campbell?"

"I noticed your photographs are numbered, and the ones I'm interested in have already been purchased."

"They are one of a kind."

"I understand your decision to exhibit a limited number of photographs in your collection, but I'm willing to pay twice as much if you—"

"I can't do that," she said, interrupting him. "The photos are part of a limited collection, and to print duplicates would be unethical. There are 120 photos in the bridges collection and not all of them have been sold. I'd like to think there are a few others you'll find to your liking."

Ivan's impassive expression revealed none of what he was feeling at that moment. "I'll give you four times the price for the triptych."

A shiver of annoyance snaked its way up Nayo's body, causing a slight shudder. "Mr. Campbell."

"It's Ivan. Please call me Ivan."

She blew out a breath. "Okay, Ivan. As I told you before, the photos are one of a kind. Perhaps you can negotiate with the person who purchased the triptych. But I cannot and will not print duplicates for you no matter how much you offer." She hesitated and exhaled a breath. "But I may be able to help you out."

"How is that?"

"I have other photos featuring bridges you may want to look at." Walking over to a side table, she picked up a small, printed card, handing it to Ivan. "This is my card. Call me and I'll set up an appointment to give you a viewing at my studio."

Reaching into the breast pocket of his jacket, Ivan removed a small silver case with his business cards. He took out a pen and wrote down his home number on the reverse side. He gave Nayo the card. "Call me and I'll make myself available."

Nayo turned the card over and read the print: Ivan G. Campbell, PhD. And, it appeared, the persistent well-dressed man was a psychotherapist. If she had to categorize his psyche, it was id-driven.

"I'll call you," she promised.

Ivan inclined his head as if she was royalty. He smiled for the first time. "I look forward to hearing from you."

Nayo held her breath. Dr. Ivan Campbell claimed the most sensual smile she'd ever seen on a man. His was a face she wanted to photograph. "You will hear from me," she said when she'd recovered her breath. Turning on her heel, she walked away from him, knowing he was staring at her.

She approached a woman who was a regular at the gallery, flashing a brittle smile and exchanging air kisses with her. "Mrs. Meyers. I hope you're enjoying the exhibit?"

Why, she thought, did she sound so specious? Had she become as plastic as some of the people who fancied themselves art collectors because it afforded them more social status?

The elderly woman waved a hand bedecked with an enormous Tahitian pearl surrounded by large, flawless diamonds. "Of course I am, darling. I bought four featuring the Natural Bridges National Monument. I can't believe you were able to photograph the night sky showing the Milky Way."

Nayo wanted to tell Mrs. Meyers that although nearly one hundred thousand people stopped at the

Natural Bridges National Monument in Utah each year, only a few took in the most breathtaking vistas, because they could only be seen at night. Whenever she visited a national park, Nayo made certain to seek out the park's chief ranger and tell him about her project. Most were more than willing to accommodate her. A few had referred to her as the female Ansel Adams. Being compared to the celebrated landscape photographer and environmentalist gave her the confidence she needed to realize her dream.

"The nighttime images were spectacular," she said, smiling.

"That's so obvious, Nayo." Mrs. Meyers waved to someone she recognized, then rushed over to talk to her, leaving Nayo to her thoughts. She'd invited her mother and father, but they hadn't been able to get away from the restaurant they'd run for more than twenty years.

Her parents had been high school sweethearts who'd married a week after graduating from college. Her father joined the local fire department while her mother had gone into teaching. Marjorie Goddard went back to work six months after giving birth to her son, but opted to become a stay-at-home mom once Nayo was born. Meanwhile her husband, Steven, had risen quickly through the ranks of the small upstate-New York fire department. Everything changed for the Goddards when Steven was injured fighting a warehouse fire. Nicknamed "Chef" by his fellow firefighters, Steven took over the cooking duties at home after having been the cook at the firehouse for so many years. He gave up fighting fires, retired and bought a run-down restaurant from an elderly couple.

What had shocked Nayo was that her parents knew nothing about the restaurant business. But after several false starts, they attracted a loyal following at the restaurant with family recipes going back several generations. What had initially been a hobby for Steven and Marjorie Goddard was now their livelihood. Just as photography had become their daughter's livelihood.

Nayo stared at Ivan Campbell. She noticed that he wasn't eating or drinking but studying her photographs. She was still staring at him when he turned and caught her. He smiled and she returned his smile with one of her own. She dropped her gaze with the approach of one of the gallery's employees.

It was hours later, when Geoff closed and locked the gallery doors, that Nayo tried recalling everything about Ivan Campbell. She didn't see him as a man who would interest her romantically, but as a subject for her next collection.

Her focus wouldn't be bridges or landscapes but people. Annie Leibovitz and Francesco Scavullo had become her idols, not only for their photographs of people but for the spirit they captured. Yes, she mused, she couldn't wait to see Ivan again if only to ask whether he would let her photograph him.

Chapter 2

Nayo climbed the stairs in the three-story East Harlem walk-up. When she'd returned from her four-year, forty-eight-state project to photograph bridges, her first choice had been to return to Greenwich Village where she'd lived while a student at New York's School of Visual Arts. However, most of the apartments she saw were either too small or too expensive. Turning her sights uptown, she'd found a large studio apartment in a renovated, three-story walk-up at Madison Avenue and 127th Street.

Geoff had offered her an apartment his family owned, but Nayo declined. It was enough that she'd lived temporarily at the beautiful St. Luke's Place row house after she'd returned to New York. It took several months for her to secure a position as a cataloger for a small Upper East Side auction house. A month later she moved to East Harlem, a neighborhood like West Harlem that was undergoing rapid gentrification.

The door to the neighboring apartment opened as Nayo put the key into her lock. A ball of smoky-colored fluff darted from between her neighbor's legs to wrap itself around Nayo's. Bending slightly, she stroked the British shorthair kitten.

"How are you, Colin?" she said softly, smiling at the friendly cat with striking copper-colored eyes. The kitten meowed softly.

When she'd asked her neighbor, Mrs. Anderson, whether she'd named her feline companion for former secretary of state Colin Powell, the retired librarian sheepishly admitted she'd formed a lasting crush on Colin Firth after watching Jane Austen's *Pride and Prejudice* over and over until she'd memorized the dialogue.

Lucille Anderson stared at the young woman who came and went inconspicuously. "I have a package for you, delivered earlier this morning."

Nayo's smile widened. "Thank you, Mrs. Anderson. As soon as I put my things down and change, I'll be over to get it."

Lucille nodded at the young woman she'd begun to

think of as the daughter she'd never had. She'd married young, but lost her husband when he suffered a massive heart attack at thirty. She'd never remarried or had children, but managed to maintain a rather active social life. She was a lifelong member of a sorority, and along with her sorors she socialized with other librarians and schoolteachers.

"Do you have time for a cup of coffee and some pound cake?"

"I'll make time," Nayo said.

Nayo had become rather attached to the woman who reminded her of her paternal grandmother. Grandma Darlene had given her the money she needed to fulfill her dream to travel coast to coast photographing bridges and whatever else caught her attention. Unfortunately her grandmother hadn't lived long enough to see her granddaughter's success. A week after she returned to New York, Nayo was sitting in her parents' living room when a call from a local hospital reported that Darlene Goddard had collapsed in a supermarket. By the time she and her parents arrived at the hospital, she was gone.

She opened the door to her apartment and Colin scooted in to jump up on a chaise where Nayo usually sat watching television. Whenever Colin came for an impromptu visit she and the kitten would cuddle together on the chaise.

"Don't get too comfortable, Colin," Nayo warned

the feline that had settled down for a nap. "I'm taking you back home as soon as I change my clothes."

Slipping out of her heels, she picked them up and placed them in a closet close to the door. She was fussy when it came to everything being in its place, because she had to eat, sleep and relax in a space measuring only 450 square feet.

A four-poster, queen-size canopy bed occupied one corner, along with an armoire, bedside tables, double dresser. A padded bench sat at the foot. A glass-topped table which doubled as a desk held a computer and printer. Nayo had stored mats and photo paper in canvas-covered baskets lined up along the wall. Her prized cameras, lenses and memory cards were in a safe in the back of the walk-in closet.

The kitchen along a brick-wall area served as her food prep and dining room. A butcher block table and four chairs covered with cushions in a sunny yellow created a cheery atmosphere for dining and entertaining.

Her small living room had a tufted sofa upholstered in the same fabric as the dining-area chairs. The coffee table was littered with art books and photography magazines. Another table against the wall held a flat-screen television and an assortment of Nayo's favorite movies. Floor lamps and strategically placed track lighting afforded the apartment a warm glow.

It took her less than fifteen minutes to remove her

makeup, apply a moisturizer and change into a long-sleeved T-shirt, jeans and a pair of running shoes. "Come, Colin," she called out, whistling and clapping her hands.

Reaching for her keys, Nayo headed for the door, the kitten trotting after her.

Ivan found his mind drifting. He had to read the same paragraph twice. He taught two classes: Clinical Use of Free Association and Dreams, and Multicultural Psychology.

The first course explored psychoanalysis dating back to Freud's study of his own patients' dreams. Course work included the introduction to current theories about dreams, empirical research on dreams and clinical work with dreams. Freud's *The Interpretation of Dreams* was required reading.

Leaning back from the desk, he stood and stretched his arms over his head. He'd spent the past four hours reading the papers of college students who, if their lives depended upon it, couldn't type a simple sentence with the correct subject and predicate agreement.

He walked out of his home office at the same time the phone rang. Retracing his steps, he picked up the receiver on the wall phone. "Hello."

"Ivan Campbell?"

His eyebrows lifted when the soft female voice came through the earpiece. "This is he."

"This is Nayo."

A smile tilted the corners of his mouth as Ivan sat on the edge of the mahogany desk. "How are you, Nayo?" He'd met her for the first time Friday evening and he hadn't expected to hear from her just two days later.

"I'm good. Thank you for asking. I'm calling because I've found quite a few prints I believe would interest you."

"Are they of bridges?"

"I have bridges and landscapes. However, before you see them I'd like to come and take a look at your home."

"When would you like to come?"

"My days and hours are flexible, so I'll leave that up to you."

Ivan glanced at the desk clock. It was minutes before noon and he had to correct two more papers before tomorrow. He taught classes on Monday and Wednesday. "I have some time this afternoon."

"Where do you live?"

He gave Nayo his address. "Where do *you* live?"

Nayo's tingling laugh came through the earpiece. "I'm within walking distance of you."

"Where do you live, Nayo?" Ivan asked again.

"I'll tell when I see you."

"When should I expect you?"

There came a pause. "I'll be over in half an hour."

"Have you—" Ivan's words trailed off when he heard Nayo had hung up. He'd just replaced the receiver when the phone rang again. "Nayo?"

"Sorry, brother, but I'm not Nayo."

"DG, what's up?"

"Don't plan anything for the first week in June."

A slight furrow appeared between Ivan's eyes. "What's going on, Duncan?"

"Tamara and I are getting married, and I'd like for you to be my best man."

Ivan went completely still. It was the second time in two months that one of his best friends had announced he was getting married. He'd met Duncan Gilmore and Kyle Chatham when they were in the same second-grade class. They also lived in the same building in a public housing complex. The three had become closer than brothers, watching one another's back. Even when Duncan's mother died and he went to live with an aunt in Brooklyn, they'd never lost touch.

Kyle and Duncan were there for him when he lost his twin brother, they attended one another's graduations, offered a shoulder when a somewhat-serious relationship ended and now, at thirty-nine, they'd fulfilled a childhood dream to own a brownstone in their Harlem neighborhood. All had worked hard to stay out of trouble when the streets had been a seductive siren, beckoning them into what would become a life of fast and easy money—and prison or certain death.

Kyle had become a lawyer, working as a corporate attorney before deciding to set up a private practice. Duncan, or DG, had made millions for clients at a Wall Street investment firm, while quietly amassing a modest fortune with his own investments.

Everything changed for Duncan when his fiancée died in the bombing of the World Trade Center. Finding himself at a crossroads, he retreated from the frenzied world of Wall Street banking and investing to set up his own company.

Ivan's career also underwent a transformation when the Washington, D.C., mental-health foundation he'd headed for years lost its funding. Ivan transferred his private patients to another therapist, sold his Georgetown home and returned to his Harlem roots.

"First the lovebug bit Kyle, now you, DG? What's going on?"

"It's all good, Ivan. I never thought I'd find someone I could love after losing Kali, but I was wrong. And I have you to thank for that."

"You came to me as a patient and not a friend, so I told you what I tell all my patients, given your circumstances. Now you and Tamara are planning a wedding."

"You didn't answer my question, Ivan."

"What's that?"

"Will you be my best man?"

"Of course I'll be your best man, DG."

"Thanks."

"Where's the wedding?" Ivan asked. Kyle and Ava Warwick had planned a Valentine's Day wedding in Puerto Rico.

"It'll be in New York. Tamara and I decided to have it on one of the yachts that sail along the Hudson River."

"I'll make certain to block out the first week in June. Congratulations and give Tamara my best."

"I'll tell her."

"Have you told Kyle you're getting married?" Ivan asked.

"I just spoke to him. He said we should set up an MNO at least once a month."

Ivan smiled. "Are you certain your woman will allow you a men's night out?" he teased.

"You're talking crazy, brother. Are you equating marriage with being on lockdown? I think you've been dating the wrong women."

"It's not about dating the wrong women, DG. It's just that I don't want to commit to one woman."

There was an uncomfortable silence before Duncan said, "You should try it, Ivan. At least once before you get too old."

"On that note, I'm going to hang up on you, Duncan. Are you going into the office tomorrow?"

"No. Tamara's off tomorrow, so we're going to look at rings."

"Let me know when you both have the same week-end off, because I'd like to host a party for you."

"I know you're not cooking, Ivan."

"Very funny, DG," he sneered. "Just because I don't grill that well doesn't mean I can't cook."

Duncan's deep chuckle came through the earpiece. "I can't eat what you grill, and I've never eaten anything you've cooked."

"On that note, I suggest you hang up, DG, or you'll find yourself looking for another best man."

"You wouldn't!"

"No, I wouldn't, DG. No matter what happens, you can count on me to be your best man." The ring of the doorbell echoed throughout the apartment. "I'm sorry, but I'm going to have to hang up on you. I'm expecting a visitor."

"I'll see you Tuesday. And thanks, Ivan."

"No problem, DG." Ivan hung up and pressed a button on the intercom. "Yes?"

"It's Nayo."

"I'll be right with you." Pressing another button, he buzzed open the lock to the outer door, and then went up the stairs to the second floor to answer the door. He hadn't expected Nayo to come so quickly.

When Ivan opened the door, he didn't realize he was staring. Nayo Goddard looked nothing like the woman he'd met at the gallery. Her fresh-scrubbed face made her look as if she were a teenage girl. She'd brushed her short hair until there was barely a hint of a curl. A black, hip-length leather jacket, turtleneck sweater, jeans and low-heeled boots had replaced her tailored blouse, skirt and heels. Nayo smiled and the dimple in her left cheek winked at him.

He returned her smile with a warm one of his own. "I'm forgetting my manners. Please come in."

Nayo realized she hadn't just imagined the sensual, brooding face of the man welcoming her into his home. Ivan Campbell wasn't what women would call a pretty brother, but he was without a doubt a very attractive man. And the stubble on his lean face served to enhance his masculinity.

The perfectly proportioned body she'd glimpsed through the cut of his suit was blatantly displayed in a white cotton pullover sweater and jeans. Instead of slip-ons, he had on running shoes.

As she stepped into the vestibule, a wave of warmth enveloped her. A mahogany staircase with carved newel posts led to the upper floors. Her gaze shifted to what appeared to be a credence table that supported a large Tiffany-style table lamp. A leather chair with decorative walnut trim complemented the furnishings in the space.

Her fingers traced the surface of the table. "Where did you get this table?"

Ivan stared openly at Nayo, whose head barely came to his shoulder. "I inherited it."

Nayo's delicate jaw dropped slightly as the notion that the table might not be a reproduction registered. "Do you mind if I ask from whom?"

"I got it from the grandmother of a former patient who lived in the D.C. area. It'd been in her family for generations."

"It's not a reproduction." Her question was a statement.

"No. It's an original. I believe it was made sometime around 1680."

Nayo stared longingly at the semicircular side table that folded out and was supported by a gateleg frame. She knew that similar antique tables were made of either walnut or oak in Britain around the second half of the seventeenth century. The space-saving tables were used in the nineteenth century to prepare the sacraments in English churches, hence the term *credence* table, which refers to church tables.

"Have you had it appraised?"

Ivan nodded. "I had to for insurance purposes."

"But why leave it out here when anyone could damage it?"

"You should've seen it before I had it restored. I was shocked when it came back looking almost like new."

Nayo traced the molding around the drawer with her fingertips. "This should be in a museum." Her head came up and she met Ivan's intense gaze. "Has anyone asked you to loan it to a museum?"

Ivan crossed his arms over his chest. "No."

"Would you if they asked?"

"I don't know."

"At least you didn't say no. Do you occupy the entire building?" Within seconds she'd changed the topic.

Reaching out, Ivan cradled her elbow. "No. I chose the street level and the second floor for my personal use. Come with me and I'll show you one of the vacant apartments on the third floor."

Nayo followed Ivan as he led her to the staircase. "What's on the top floor?"

"You'll see," he said cryptically. "By the way, how did you get here so fast?"

"I live on 127th Street off Madison."

Ivan released her elbow to take her hand, giving her fingers a gentle squeeze. "We're practically neighbors."

"How long have you lived here?" Nayo asked.

"Not too long. I bought this place three years ago. It took about a year and a half to renovate."

She noted the parquet flooring along the third-floor hallway. "It looks as if you restored it."

Ivan gave the talented photographer a sidelong glance. "I suppose I should've said it took that long to restore it. The architect managed to find photographs of another brownstone similar to this one, and he knew exactly what it looked like before the former owners made changes."

"What updates did you make?"

"You'll see when I show you the apartment."

Ivan led Nayo down the hallway to the rear of the brownstone and opened a door to a vacant apartment.

It was at Duncan's urging that he decided to rent out the apartments. The accountant told him that the rental income would offset the expense of renovating the four-story structure.

He'd bought the abandoned brownstone outright with the proceeds from the sale of his D.C. home. He'd taken out a loan for the renovations, because he hadn't wanted to exhaust his savings and have a cash-flow problem. Although he hadn't wanted to be saddled with a mortgage, it was unavoidable when he, Duncan and Kyle purchased another brownstone in the same historic district. He would've found it stressful to carry two mortgages on two pieces of property. Luckily he and his friends purchased property when interest rates and house prices were still relatively low, and despite the mortgage-and-housing crisis, he, Kyle and Duncan were in good stead financially.

He couldn't charge his patients the fees other therapists did, which was why he supplemented his income with teaching and private lectures. One of his ongoing personal projects was writing a couple of books—one a humanistic view of multicultural psychology, the other psychology and African-Americans.

Opening the door, Ivan stepped aside to let Nayo walk in. "This apartment is the same as the one at the front of the building."

An entryway with gleaming hardwood floors in a herringbone design led to a living room with a trio of floor-to-ceiling windows. A raised area for dining over-looked the expansive living room. Nayo walked through the dining area to a gourmet kitchen with top-of-the line appliances and a black-and-white tile floor.

"Each apartment has a full bath and half bath," Ivan said behind her.

"This place is beautiful," she said reverently.

And it was. Nayo didn't know how much Ivan was charging for rent, but if she'd seen the apartment first, she would've paid whatever he'd asked. High ceilings with recessed lighting, exquisite wood floors and natural light coming through the tall windows.

Ivan reached for her hand, cradling it gently in his protective grasp. "The half bath is off the kitchen, and the bedrooms are over here," he said, leading her across the living room.

Nayo entered the master bedroom with its en suite bath. The bath had a freestanding shower and a Jacuzzi garden bathtub. The smaller bedroom, although spa-cious, lacked an adjoining bath. Solar shades that let light in without sacrificing privacy covered all the windows, and the bedroom floors were covered in car-peting in an oatmeal shade.

"Now the top floor."

Ivan led Nayo up the staircase to the fourth floor. He'd thought of putting in an elevator, but changed his mind, because he wasn't certain what he wanted to do with the top floor. Carved double mahogany doors opened to a yawning space with brick walls, cherry-wood floors, floor-to-ceiling windows and a coffered ceiling.

"What do you plan to put up here?"

"I haven't decided yet."

Nayo tried analyzing the man standing less than a foot away. It was only their second encounter, yet she felt very comfortable with him. It'd been that way when she'd met Geoffrey Magnus for the first time. She hadn't had a lot of experience with men, with the exception of an intense summer romance the year she graduated from high school. She'd dated, although casually, but had yet to experience a passionate affair.

She knew her reluctance to get involved with a man stemmed from her desire to focus on establishing a career as a professional photographer. Taking pictures wasn't a frivolous hobby or a passing fancy, but a passion. From the first time she held a camera she was hooked, and the obsession continued unabated.

"What I've seen is incredible. I see why a magazine would want to do a photo spread of your home."

"I owe it all to a very talented architect and interior designer."

Nayo gave Ivan a sidelong glance. "Don't be so modest, Ivan. After all, you did have to approve the plans and the furnishings."

"I suppose you're right."

"I know I'm right," she countered. "It's the same

when I take a shot. I know within seconds whether I've captured the image I want or I have to reshoot it."

Resting his hand at the small of Nayo's back, Ivan steered her toward the staircase. "How many pictures did you take to come up with the 120 in your bridge collection?"

"I have more than 120 photographs in my bridge collection."

Ivan stopped before stepping off at the second floor landing. "I thought you said the exhibition was a limited collection."

"I said the photographs in that collection will not be reprinted. I have others that I'll show probably in a couple of years. If I decide never to exhibit them, then I'll include them in a coffee-table book."

"Do you have photos of any of the New York City bridges?"

Nayo nodded. "I have several of the Brooklyn Bridge at different times of the day."

"Hot damn!" he said under his breath.

The skin around Nayo's eyes crinkled when she laughed, the soft, sensual sound bubbling up from her throat. Ivan's deep, rumbling laugh joined hers, and they were still laughing when he opened the door to his apartment to give her a tour of what had become a designer's show house.

Chapter 3

Reaching into her jacket pocket, Nayo removed a small, handheld video recorder. She hadn't realized her hand was shaking until she tried to take off her jacket. The rumors she'd heard about Carla Harris's meteoric rise in the world of interior design were true, as evidenced by the blending of textures and colors. The interior of Ivan Campbell's duplex was breathtakingly beautiful.

"I'll take that," Ivan said, reaching for Nayo's jacket. "You can either start here or downstairs."

Nayo stared at the area off the entryway, which contained a leather grouping in front of a minimalist-designed fireplace. "I'd like to see the rooms alone."

Her gaze shifted to Ivan, seeing an expression of confusion on his handsome face. "I like to feel the space, and I can't do that if there's someone else there with me. Rooms, if they aren't empty, are like people, Ivan," she explained softly. "Each one has a personality based on the color of the walls, flooring, the window treatments and the furnishings. It's the same when I study a subject or object I plan to photograph. It's not about looking through a camera lens and snapping the image. It's seeing beyond that. That's the difference between an amateur and professional photographer."

Ivan inclined his head in agreement. He'd had a patient who was an artist, and he was more than familiar with his quirky personality. Despite having a successful career, he never believed in himself. After being commissioned to paint a mural for the lobby of a major corporation, he'd spend months procrastinating. Fear and self-doubt brought on a paralyzing anxiety that made it almost impossible for him to pick up a brush. Following a series of intense therapy sessions, he worked nonstop to make the deadline. If Nayo needed solitude, he'd comply with her request.

"Take your time."

Nayo exhaled inaudibly. She thought Ivan wouldn't agree to her going through his home unaccompanied, because the first time she'd made a similar request to a potential client, she'd found herself ushered out of the woman's Sutton Place penthouse—but not before Nayo told her there wasn't anything in her apartment worth stealing and going to jail for.

Smiling, she winked at Ivan. "I'll be back."

"Would you like a café latte or cappuccino?"

"I'd love a latte, thank you."

"Would you like it now or when you're finished?"

"I'll have it when I'm finished."

Nayo was anxious to tour the house so she could recommend photographs that would be suitable for the magazine spread. Ivan hadn't mentioned the name of the magazine, but she knew it was *Architectural Digest.* When Carla Harris attended the preview showing, she'd babbled incessantly about how the preeminent interior-design magazine wanted to photograph the home of one of her clients.

Switching on the tape recorder, she spoke quietly into the speaker. "I've just passed an alcove with a leather grouping in butter-yellow designed for small, intimate gatherings in front of a minimalist fireplace. There is no fireplace mantel, but a grouping of shadow boxes would break up the starkness of the oyster-white wall."

She continued into the living room, where a neutral palette of white, cream and tan provided an elegant backdrop for comfort and elegance. Nayo felt the room was a little too formal with a tufted, brown-leather sofa, chairs and doubled-tiered, beveled-glass coffee table positioned at an angle on the cream-colored plush rug.

Switching on the recorder again, she said, "There are

books, a chess set with full-leaded crystal pieces on the coffee table. There's a Waterford lamp on a side table, along with a Waterford Crystal 2000 World Series Home Plate New York City Subway Series collectible. Dr. Ivan Campbell likes music, sports and chess."

Nayo lost track of time as she entered and left rooms that bore the designer's distinctive mark. Carla Harris had made her reputation by incorporating the personality of the owner within the space's function. Unlike Ivan, she wasn't a psychologist, but what Nayo saw spoke volumes. He was a chameleon, switching flawlessly from formal to informal with a change of attire.

Friday night he was Dr. Campbell. She'd found him somewhat passive-aggressive when he'd tried to talk her into duplicating the prints he wanted. It was only when she stood her ground that he backed off. Sunday afternoon he was Ivan, welcoming, cooperative and amenable to her suggestions.

It took Nayo less than half an hour to ascertain that Ivan wasn't married. Everything in his house was as masculine as he, and nowhere was there anything feminine—no intimate products, hairdressing, perfume or deodorant on the dressing tables in any of the bathrooms. His home was the proverbial bachelor pad.

The master bedroom projected a Zen quality: platform bed with gray, black and white accessories. The minimalist Asian decor was carried over into the bath with two large, pale green bowls doubling as basins and a matching garden tub with enough space for four adults.

The furnishings in the three guest bedrooms were reminiscent of Caribbean plantation homes under British Colonial rule. The mosquito netting draping the four-poster beds reminded Nayo of her own bed, with its mosquito netting embroidered with tiny yellow pineapples.

Walking through the formal dining room with a magnificent crystal chandelier over a table with seating for ten, she found herself in a state-of-the-art, gourmet kitchen. Pots, pans and utensils were suspended from a rack over a cooking island. Her gaze swept over a subzero refrigerator, wine cellar and a collection of cookbooks on a shelf near an espresso machine.

Nayo walked through the kitchen into a well-stocked pantry, then a laundry room, then down a flight of stairs to the street level. She pushed a button on the recorder. "Framed movie prints would work well on the walls of the home theater. I'm leaving the home theater and walking into a home office. There are two photographs of Malcolm X, the only photos in the entire apartment. One is a candid shot and the other a framed print issued by the U.S. Postal Service. Black-and-white landscapes will work well in the home office." She turned off the recorder.

The utility kitchen, with its stainless-steel appliances, and a glass-and-porcelain bathroom needed no additional adornment. Nayo smiled when she walked into the gym. Ivan's toned body was a testament to the fact that he made good use of the workout bench and assorted weights, a rowing machine and a heavy punching bag suspended from the ceiling by a chain.

She crossed the room and opened the door to a steam room. It was apparent Ivan Campbell had everything he needed to make his life as stress-free as possible. She retreated up the staircase to the gourmet kitchen at the same time Ivan walked in.

"Are you ready for your latte?"

Nayo nodded as she sat on a tall stool at a counter adjacent to the cooking island. "Yes, please."

His eyebrows lifted in question. "What do you think of the apartment?" he asked as he filled a grinder with coffee beans.

"I love it," she replied truthfully, "and it's certainly worthy of a magazine layout."

"I have Carla to thank for that."

"Don't be so modest, Ivan. I'm sure you had some input."

"A little," he admitted with a sheepish grin.

"It was more than a little," Nayo admonished in a soft tone. "I know you like movies, working out, playing the piano, chess, baseball and cooking."

Ivan made a face. "You're right about everything but the cooking."

"What's up with the cookbooks?"

"I'm trying to teach myself to cook."

"Why don't you take a few classes?"

"I would," he said, "but I don't have the time. I have my private practice and I teach classes two days a week."

Ivan decided to experiment with cooking after his best friends refused to eat his food. He'd accepted that his grilling methods were less than stellar, but he hadn't done too badly on the stove top or baking. The night before, he'd made spaghetti carbonara, following the recipe to the letter, and the result was amazing. He wanted to wait until he'd perfected a few more dishes, then invite Kyle, Duncan and their respective fiancées for dinner.

He couldn't believe that his best friends' summer romances hadn't ended with the end of the season, but would continue beyond the time when they exchanged vows. He'd be best man at both their weddings.

Despite setting up their respective businesses in the same building, they got together less often than when they were employees of other companies. Even when he lived and worked in D.C., Ivan would drive up to New York several times a month to reconnect with his childhood friends.

He, Duncan and Kyle had vowed years ago they would always remain connected even if separated by thousands of miles. And although they did not share DNA, they were brothers in the truest sense of the word.

"What are your favorite movies?" Nayo asked, breaking into his reverie.

Ivan's gaze narrowed. "I don't know."

"Don't you have at least three or four favorites you've seen more than once?"

He pushed a button and the fragrant aroma of coffee filled the kitchen. "I'm somewhat partial to *Glory, Witness, The Godfather* and *The Departed*. Why do you want to know?"

Nayo smiled. Ivan had named two of her favorite films. He liked heavy drama. "I'd like to order archival movie posters for the walls of your home theater. Now if you have a few black-and-white favorites, I'll see if they, too, can be ordered. The contrast between the classic movies and what will become new classics will bring a nice touch to the room. If you decide you don't want them matted and framed, they can be bonded to a board using a thermal heating process. Another option is to set them up on easels. Either way the posters will add warmth and personality to the space."

Talented, intelligent and beautiful, Ivan mused. "Are you certain you'll be able to get those?"

Resting her elbows on the marble-topped counter, Nayo leaned forward. "I know someone in the business."

"I guess it all goes back to who you know, not what you know," he quipped.

"Sometimes it's both. I went to college with a guy whose father is a Hollywood still photographer."

Ivan emptied the finely ground coffee into the well of

the coffee machine, added water and then pushed a button for the brewing cycle. "Which college did you attend?"

"The School of Visual Arts."

"When did you graduate?"

A knowing smile softened Nayo's features. "Are you asking because you want to know how much experience I have in the field, or are you asking because you want to know how old I am?"

Ivan went completely still. It was apparent Nayo saw through his ruse. Not many people could read him that well. "Okay, you got me. How old are you, Nayo?"

Resting her chin on the heel of her hand, she made a sensual moue, bringing his gaze to linger on her mouth. "I'm thirty-one."

"You had me fooled," Ivan admitted. "I thought you were at least ten years younger."

"I guess there's some truth in the saying 'Black don't crack.'"

Ivan assumed a similar pose when he rested his elbows inches from hers. "I'd attribute it more to a good gene pool."

Nayo lifted her shoulders. "It could be a combination of the two. Since you've asked me a very personal question, I'm going to return the favor. How old are you?"

Attractive lines fanned out around his eyes when he smiled, a smile she yearned to capture for posterity. "I'm thirty-nine." He'd celebrated a birthday earlier that spring.

"You don't look that old."

"How *old* do I look?"

"Younger than thirty-nine," Nayo said.

"How many thirty-nine-year-old men have you known?"

"I haven't known as many as I've seen. I'm a photographer, Ivan, so whenever I meet someone, my first instinct is to study their face. And yours is a very interesting face."

Ivan gave Nayo a long, penetrating stare. He'd been called a lot of things, but he couldn't remember anyone referring to him as *interesting*. The seconds ticked off as they stared at each other.

"Did I embarrass you, Dr. Campbell?"

"No," he countered. "And please don't call me Dr. Campbell. You're not my student or my patient."

Nayo nodded, but didn't drop her gaze. "Point taken," she said. "I think the coffee's ready for my latte."

Ivan leaned closer. "To be continued."

His comment told Nayo more than she wanted to know about the psychotherapist. He didn't like conceding. She stared at the breadth of his shoulders under the cotton pullover. "Will you allow me to photograph you?" It was a question that had nagged at her since she'd come face-to-face with Ivan at the gallery.

Ivan's hand didn't waver as he poured a small amount of steaming, frothy milk into a cup of black coffee.

Carrying the cup and napkin, he placed them on the counter in front of her. "Why do want to photograph me?"

"Aren't you going to make a cup for yourself?"

"No. I've already had three cups today, and that's my limit."

Her eyebrows rose. "That's a lot of coffee."

Ivan nodded. "I'm down from six cups a day. Why do you want to photograph me?" he asked again.

"I like your face."

"It's interesting," he teased.

Nayo winked at him. "Very. Your features are very symmetrical, and you have what I think of as a beguiling smile. It's warm, inviting and as a woman I find it quite sensual. You also have beautiful hands."

"Stop it, Nayo. I thank you for your glowing assessment, but I can't."

"I'll pay you, Ivan."

"It's not about money."

"What is it about, then?"

"I don't want or need my face on display at some gallery. I'm a therapist and teacher, not some celebrity."

"But you *are* a celebrity, Dr. Campbell," Nayo argued softly. "Are you aware of how many sites come up when your name is searched on Google? Thirty-eight," she said when he gave her an impassive stare. "Don't worry, Ivan, I won't sell your photograph."

"What do you plan to do with it?"

"Use it in a retrospective."

"That's it?"

She smiled. "That's it, Ivan. And I would stipulate this when you sign a release."

Ivan shook his head. "I don't know, Nayo. I have to think about it."

She wanted to ask him what there was to think about. Most people she knew would jump at the opportunity to have their photographs taken by a professional photographer. She'd spent four years photographing bridges, and now her focus had become people— people from every race, ethnic group and every walk of life. The world was her canvas and she planned to fill every inch of it.

She forced a smile she didn't feel. "At least you didn't say no."

"But I could," Ivan countered.

A shiver of annoyance shook her. It was the second time in two days that Ivan Campbell had her close to losing her temper. "Either it's yes or no, Ivan, because I'm not into playing games."

Ivan bared his beautiful white teeth. "I told you I have to think about it."

"Dial down the bully-boy attitude. You don't frighten me."

A slow smile crinkled the skin around his eyes. "It wasn't my intent to frighten you."

Nayo drew the back of her hand over her forehead,

mimicking a gesture of relief. "Whew! For a moment I thought you were going to put me under the bright lights and pull out the rubber hose."

Throwing back his head, Ivan laughed loudly. "Either you're overly dramatic or you've been watching too many old police-procedural movies."

She gave him a bright smile. "I've always had a secret desire to act."

Ivan sobered. "You'd be a very beautiful actress."

Two pairs of dark eyes met and fused as a beat passed. Nayo broke the visual impasse when she picked up her cup, staring at Ivan over the rim, and took a sip of lukewarm coffee.

"What's the matter, Nayo? Cat got your tongue?"

She dabbed her mouth with the napkin. "No," she answered softly.

"I just paid you a compliment."

"Was it a compliment, or are you flirting with me?"

"Both."

Nayo recoiled visibly. It wasn't often she met someone as honest and in-your-face as Ivan Campbell, and she wondered if it was because of his profession. "Do you flirt with every woman you meet?"

"No."

"You are flirting, yet you know nothing about me. I could be married."

"But you're not married, Nayo."

Her eyes narrowed. "How would you know that?"

A mysterious smile played at the corners of Ivan's mouth. "You're not the only one who's Internet savvy. It was after I went through the catalog of your work at the gallery that I came home and searched your name. I seriously doubt any normal man would permit his wife to be away from him for four years while she indulged in her obsession to photograph every conceivable natural or manmade bridge."

"You think of photography as an obsession?"

"Not the profession in and of itself. But to be away from home and all that's familiar for years doesn't quite fall within the normal range."

Resting her chin on the heel of her hand, Nayo smiled at Ivan. "Are you attempting to psychoanalyze me, Dr. Campbell?"

He leaned closer and the fragrance of his cologne on warmed flesh tantalized her olfactory sense. The man in whose kitchen she sat claimed the winning combination of looks, brains and professional success. *If* she'd been interested in looking for someone with whom to have a relationship, Ivan would've been the perfect candidate. However, she didn't need or want a man, because any emotional entanglement would conflict with her career. She was only thirty-one, her biological clock wasn't ticking and she had a lot of time ahead of her for love, marriage and children.

Ivan ran a finger down the length of her short,

delicate nose. "No. I don't want to know *that* much about you. I find it more intriguing to find out things over time."

"How much time are you talking about?"

"That depends on the woman."

"Why," Nayo whispered, "are you being so evasive?"

Ivan winked. "I thought I was being *miss-steery-ous*," he drawled in what sounded to Nayo like an Eastern European accent.

"You are so silly," Nayo countered. "You need to have your head examined." She sobered quickly. "Now, back to why I'm here. I have a collection of photographs you can use for your living room, master bedroom, bath, living and dining rooms. I'm not so certain about the guest bedrooms. You may have to look elsewhere for something that will conform to the decor."

"What are you thinking of?"

"I'd like to see ferns, flowers and birds reminiscent of Audubon prints, in keeping with the tropical theme."

"Where would I find them?"

"I'll get them for you. Chances are I'll be able to come up with some quicker than you can, and probably at a better price. And if it's all right with you, I'll buy the prints and mats and frame them myself. That also will lower the cost considerably."

Ivan waved a hand. "Don't worry about how much

they cost. If you'll give me an approximate amount of what you think they'll come to, I'll write you a check."

Nayo shook her head. "That's not necessary. The people I deal with will bill me."

"What about your commission?"

"What about it, Ivan?"

"How much commission do you want?"

Unconsciously Nayo furrowed her brow. She'd put herself into the position of becoming his agent or representative. "Five percent." It was the first figure to come to mind. She would sell him her photographs, but there was no way she was going to rip him off when she negotiated for the prints for the bedrooms.

"Aren't the prevailing rates for agents between fifteen and twenty-five percent?"

"Don't forget I'm going to charge you for the photos, matting and framing."

"When do you want me to look at the photos?"

"That's up to you," Nayo said.

"What if I come to the gallery on Friday?"

Ivan had made it a practice not to schedule patients on Friday. The only exception was an emergency, and thankfully he hadn't had too many of those. He lectured Monday and Wednesday morning, then saw patients in the afternoon and evening. He was available all day Tuesday and Thursday for scheduled appointments and walk-ins, and had set aside Thursdays as his late night.

"I'm sorry, but the gallery is closed on Friday, unless there is a showing."

He exhaled. "I teach and see patients every day of the week except Friday."

Nayo pondered Ivan's scheduling dilemma. She worked Monday, Wednesday and Friday at the auction house and toured the different neighborhoods on Tuesday looking for subjects to photograph. Her Thursdays were spent cleaning her apartment, shopping for food and dropping off and picking up laundry.

"I can see you on Friday, but it will have to be after six," she said, knowing she had to compromise to give Ivan what he needed for the magazine layout.

"So I'll meet you at the gallery?" Ivan asked.

A beat passed. "I'm not sure. I'll let you know."

Nayo knew if she couldn't convince Geoff to open the gallery for her to use for a few hours on Friday, then Ivan would have to come to her apartment. No male, other than her father and brother, had crossed the threshold to what she'd come to think of as her sanctuary. It was there where she went to eat, sleep, relax and examine the shots she'd taken during her block-by-block walking expedition, and not entertain men.

She and Geoff had an explosive interchange when he'd called out of the blue, asking to drop by. She'd tried explaining that she was raised never to drop in on someone without an invitation, but Geoff was quite vocal when he said her protocol was not only rigid, but archaic. His reference to her upstate roots was like waving a red flag in front of a bull, and several weeks passed before she would take his calls. He apologized profusely and never broached the subject again.

"What if we meet over dinner?" Ivan asked.

"Are you cooking?" she teased.

Straightening, Ivan angled his head. "You really want me to cook?"

Pushing to her feet, Nayo waved her hands. "Why do you sound so surprised? You have a kitchen to die for with all the accoutrements, and you have the audacity to ask me whether I want you to cook. Of course I do," she said, enunciating each word.

Ivan made a face. "I'm really not that good."

Suddenly Ivan recalled the spaghetti carbonara he'd prepared. "I'll cook," he said, smiling. "Do you like Italian?"

Her expression brightened. "I love it."

"Are you lactose-intolerant?"

Nayo shook her head. "No. Do you mind if I bring dessert?" Ivan flashed the smile she wanted to capture for posterity. Somehow she had to get him to agree to sit for her.

"Of course not. Call me and let me know what time you want me to pick you up."

"That's not necessary."

"Yes, it is."

"I live practically around the corner."

"Even if you lived next door I'd still come and pick you up. The days are getting shorter and by six it's starting to get dark."

Nayo knew she had to *play nice* with Ivan, because she wanted to shoot him. "Okay. I'll call you when I'm ready and you can come and get me. Thank you for the latte."

There was just enough sarcasm in her tone to make Ivan give her a pointed look. Pretending she didn't notice it, she turned on her heel and walked out of the kitchen, Ivan following. He picked up her jacket off the chair in the alcove, holding it while she slipped her arms into the sleeves.

"Don't leave yet," Ivan warned as he opened the door to a closet off the entryway. Reaching for a lightweight windbreaker, he put it on, then opened the drawer in the credence table and took out a set of keys. "Now I'm ready."

"Ready for what?"

"To walk you home."

Nayo gave the man with the superinflated ego a baleful look that spoke volumes. Yes, he was gorgeous, educated, owned a beautiful home and apparently was solvent, but that didn't translate into her gushing over him as if he were the last man on the face of the earth.

She knew her youthful appearance shocked a lot of people, but she wasn't a girl. She'd had a long-term relationship that ended in a broken engagement; she'd spent several summers in Europe, avoiding the advances of men who saw her as easy prey; and she'd put more than one hundred thousand miles on her car when she'd crisscrossed the continental United States shooting more than a thousand pictures.

Ivan had admitted he'd been flirting with her, but Nayo Cassandra Goddard wasn't biting. Growing her career, not becoming involved with a man, had become her priority.

"I'm not going home. I'm meeting someone for dinner." She'd made plans to meet Geoff at a seafood restaurant on the Upper East Side. "I'll call you," she said cheerfully.

Ivan nodded numbly like a bobble-head doll. Nayo was there and then she wasn't as the door closed quietly behind her departing figure. He'd detected a subtle defiance in the photographer, defiance he saw as a challenge.

Many of the women he'd dated failed to hold his interest for more than a few weeks, but there was something about the petite photographer that intrigued him, intrigued him enough to want to see her again.

He hadn't realized that until he'd opened the door to find her standing there. Ivan knew he could've asked Carla to purchase or rent the requisite art, but after seeing Nayo's photos and meeting her, he realized he didn't want or need Carla's involvement.

He liked Nayo, but what he had to uncover was why.

What was it about her that made her different from other women?

And how had a little slip of a woman managed to get to the man who'd earned the reputation of "love them and leave them"?

Nayo hadn't outright rejected his advances, but Ivan knew she wasn't going to be easy. And that was the difference between her and other women—they'd been too easy.

Chapter 4

Ivan picked up a piece of chalk and began drawing and labeling columns on the chalkboard. "Today we're going to talk about culturally mediated belief and practices as they pertain to different racial and ethnic groups. We're going to cover five ethnic groups—Russian, Native American, Mexican, Asian and African-Americans. Each group, although American, relates differently to birth and dying, religion, role differences and communication."

Turning, he stared at the students staring back at him. The course was open only to juniors and seniors, and was a favorite of Ivan's; the dozen students came to class with the intent to challenge him at every turn.

A male student who'd bleached his jet-black hair a shocking flaxen color raised his hand. "Dr. Campbell?"

Ivan turned, noticing that the young man had applied black polish to his nails. "Yes, Mr. Hernandez?"

"You have Mexicans, but you didn't include Puerto Ricans."

"We'll discuss them separately. With more than four hundred ethno-cultural groups it is virtually impossible to cover every group in North America. As therapists it is incumbent on you to familiarize yourself with the customs and characteristics of most of the groups you'll work with. Sensitivity to any customs that aren't your own will determine how effective you'll be with your patients. I always require an ethno-cultural assessment during the intake process."

"What are some of the questions on the form?" asked a female student who always came to class with her head and body covered.

"Don't be afraid to ask the patient their ethnic origin, the primary language spoken at home or if they require an interpreter. Religious beliefs, restrictions and practices are important for understanding and perception of mental-health therapy."

"I am Muslim, so how does dying differ from someone who is African-American and Christian?"

Ivan moved over and sat on the edge of the desk. He never liked the traditional classroom seating, so he had his students rearrange their chairs in a U formation.

"Muslims believe death is God's will," Ivan replied. "They always turn a patient's bed to face the East, or Mecca, and read from the Koran. There are no cremations or autopsies. The only exception would be for forensics and organ donations.

"African-Americans are reluctant to donate their organs, and family members will usually make the decision when it comes to the deceased. Their response to death is varied, so you may get a lot of different ones. Funerals and burials may take as long as five days to a week after death. It is very important to ascertain the patient's religious affiliation during the interview process and know the importance of religion or church in his or her life."

Ivan made certain not to make eye contact with his Muslim student. He'd learned that some females avoided eye contact with males and strangers. He wasn't a stranger, but he was male. "Islam instructs you to pray five times each day, fast during Ramadan and take a pilgrimage to Mecca at least once during your lifetime."

He gave the students an overview of the ethnocultural differences before giving each a handout of the assessment tool. This was Ivan's first year teaching a humanistic view of a course that covered selected psychological literature on non-white Americans, and most of the data was derived from his published doctoral dissertation.

A lively discussion ensued until Ivan glanced at his watch, noting he'd gone ten minutes beyond the time for dismissal. "For those of you who have another class, you'd better hustle or you're going to be late. Have a good weekend, and I'll see you Monday."

He gathered the extra handouts, slipping them into a leather case, then checked his cell phone. Someone had sent him a voice-mail message. Punching in his PIN, he listened to the soft, feminine voice coming through the earpiece.

It was Nayo, and this was the first time he detected an inflection in her speech pattern that was different from those living in New York City. Pressing a button, he replayed her message: *Ivan, this is Nayo. Please call me when you get this message.* She left the numbers for her cell, home and work.

Ivan wrote down the numbers, then dialed the one for her cell. "This is Ivan," he said after hearing her soft greeting.

"Oh, Ivan, I'm so sorry, but I'm going to have to cancel Friday. I just remembered that a friend is hosting a pre-Halloween party and I promised her I would attend."

"What costume are you wearing?"

"Costumes are optional. Is it possible for us to meet tonight?"

"I can't give you an answer until I check with my office. Hang up and I'll call you back."

Ivan had purposely kept busy so he wouldn't have

to think about Nayo Goddard, but just hearing her voice again conjured up the image of her doll-like, wide-eyed gaze. He didn't know why, but he remembered every curve of her petite body as if she were standing in front of him. He dialed his office, counting off the rings until his secretary answered the call. It rang six times, followed by a distinctive click that indicated the call had been transferred to the reception desk.

"Counseling Center, Demetria speaking. How may I direct your call?"

"Demetria, this is Ivan. Can you check my calendar and tell me who's scheduled to come in this afternoon?"

He, Duncan and Kyle had set up a synchronized computer program where the building's reception desk knew all their schedules at a glance. His offices took up the top floor in the renovated brownstone, Kyle's law practice the second floor and Duncan's tax-and-financial services the first floor. The street-level space was converted to include a kitchen, dining room, games room and gym for the building's employees. He shared equally in the salaries for the receptionists and cleaning staff.

"You had Ahmed Daniels for five, but he called to say he had to meet with his probation officer."

"Did he reschedule?"

"No, Dr. Campbell."

"Leave a message for Chantal to call Ahmed and reschedule ASAP."

"Chantal didn't come in today. She called to say she

had a fight with her baby's daddy last night, and he wouldn't take care of Kassim, so she had to try to find another babysitter."

Chantal came with excellent office skills, but it was her personal life that was in disarray. Her on-again, off-again relationship with her son's father was beginning to affect her job performance. Her punctuality and attendance had received a less than favorable rating on her last evaluation.

"Don't schedule anyone else for today, and if there is an emergency, refer them either to Dr. Kelly or the hospital. What does Thursday look like?"

"You have a full calendar. Your first appointment is at ten and your last is scheduled for eight."

Originally Ivan had set aside Tuesday for his late night, but then switched to Thursdays because patients tended not to keep their Friday appointments, which prompted him to work late and take Fridays off.

"If Chantal calls, please tell her that I must talk to her before I go into session tomorrow morning."

"Okay, Dr. Campbell."

Ivan hung up, then called Nayo back. "I'm free for tonight."

"What time do you want to get together?"

"I'm still at the college. It should take me about half an hour to get home."

"Why don't I plan to see you in, say, an hour and a half?"

"That works fine," he agreed.

"Ivan?"

"Yes, Nayo."

"You don't have to cook."

He affected a Cheshire-cat grin. "What if I order in?"

"That'll work. I'll see you ninety minutes."

Ivan pressed a button, ending the call. He would get to see Nayo sooner than planned, but there was still the problem with his secretary he had to resolve. Chantal's salary was comparable to someone working for a major downtown corporation, because she was the sole support for herself and her son. The young woman complained that her son's father was unemployed, so he wasn't able to contribute to the child's support. The man supposedly made up for his lack of funds by babysitting the child when his mother was at work. Now that that arrangement had soured, Ivan knew it was time for Chantal to see about enrolling two-year-old Kassim in day care. Either she followed through with his recommendation, or he would be forced to terminate her employment.

Unlike Duncan and Kyle, he ran a bare-bones practice. An intern enrolled in the psychology program at City University New York's Graduate Center came in twice a week to do intakes and assessments. Chantal was responsible for scheduling, inputting case notes and following up with patients mandated by schools and the court-and-criminal-justice system.

Kyle and his law partner, Jordan Wainwright, had expanded their thriving practice, adding a law clerk to a staff that included an office manager and full- and part-time paralegals.

Duncan Gilmore, his part-time accounting student and full-time executive assistant had established a reputation in the Harlem community based on good faith and honesty.

Ivan teased Duncan that he never had to worry about an IRS audit or losing his investments to fraudulent trading, because he had him monitoring his resources. Projected income from his private counseling practice was far below what Kyle and Duncan derived from their firms, but his year-end revenue was comparable because of the income from renting the apartments, his position as an adjunct professor and his speaking engagements.

He was still trying to wrap his head around the fact that Kyle would marry Ava in February, and Duncan his doctor-girlfriend in June. They would become husbands and fathers, leaving him to take on the role as godfather to their children.

Despite having dated a lot of women, Ivan could honestly say that he hadn't slept with a lot of them. For him a physical entanglement was tantamount to an emotional commitment. And for those he did sleep with he was forthcoming when he told them that he wasn't the marrying kind. Some accepted it, and many didn't.

Most women he knew wanted to marry and have children. He'd found himself drawn to those who professed they didn't want marriage and motherhood.

Ivan knew that his reluctance to form a permanent bond with a woman came from his losing his twin. Not only had he and Jared been identical in appearance, they'd had an uncanny ability to read each other's mind. They'd played jokes on family members and teachers when they switched identities. The only one they couldn't fool was their mother, Winnifred Campbell. Winnie, as she was affectionately called, had decided from the moment she was told she'd given birth to identical twin boys that she wouldn't give them names that sounded alike or even began with the same letter, and that she would never dress them alike. When he asked his mother how she could tell them apart when their own father couldn't, Winnie said it was a *mother thing*.

It wasn't until after they'd buried Jared that Winnie told Ivan that she saw something in Jared that was missing in him—trust. Jared had always been quick to smile or tell a joke. He'd been more outgoing and willing to befriend someone, while Ivan had remained aloof. Jared had always had more friends than Ivan, but unfortunately following his friends had gotten Jared killed.

Picking up a lightweight raincoat, Ivan slipped it on over his suit. When he'd gotten up earlier that morning, meteorologists were predicting rain, with temperatures in the low forties. Fall had come and he'd looked forward to an Indian summer. Halloween was five days away and the temperature had dropped steadily with the waning daylight hours.

Grasping his leather case, he tucked it under his arm and left the classroom. He hadn't planned to teach, but a former professor had asked him to fill in for a colleague taking a sabbatical. The first time he walked into the classroom and introduced himself as Dr. Campbell, he felt as if he belonged there. It'd taken years for him to go from a college freshman not knowing what he wanted to study to graduating with an honors degree in the social sciences.

He attended graduate school as a psychology major, then followed as a postgraduate, working toward a PhD. He took a year off before enrolling in a postdoctoral program in psychotherapy and psychoanalysis. His sister, Roberta, teased him, saying he'd become a professional student, but the education and training had given him expert status in his field when it came to understanding the psyche of African-American youth.

Ivan stepped out onto the sidewalk and was met with an onslaught of icy pellets. The rain had turned to sleet. Turning up the collar of his raincoat, he ducked his head and walked toward the West Fourth Street-Washington Square subway station.

Nayo rang the bell to Ivan's brownstone, chiding herself for walking, instead of taking a cab. The temperature was just above freezing, but with the sleet it felt colder. "It's Nayo," she said into the small intercom speaker affixed to the side of the building when she heard Ivan's smooth baritone ask who it was. There came a buzzing sound and she pushed open the door and stepped into the cloaking warmth of the vestibule. She smiled when she saw a pair of men's shoes on a thick straw mat under the credence table. Sitting in the leather chair, she bent over to take off her boots at the same time the door to Ivan's apartment opened.

Her head came up and she met his mesmerizing smile. He looked as if he was dressed for the tropics: colorful Hawaiian shirt, khaki walking shorts and sandals.

"Hi."

Ivan winked at Nayo. "Hi. Come in where it's warm."

Standing, she placed her shoes on the mat, then walked into the apartment. The air throughout the entryway was redolent with the sweet, fragrant smell of burning wood. Shrugging out of her coat, she handed it to Ivan.

Hoisting a leather tote over her shoulder, she rubbed her palms together. "It feels good in here."

Ivan closed the closet door and turned to Nayo. She hadn't worn gloves or a hat, and moisture shimmered on her curly hair like diamond dust. Reaching for her hands, he cradled them. "Where are your gloves?"

Nayo met the gaze of the man whose image she couldn't get out of her head. She was fascinated not only by his face but also the man himself. And did he look good. He also smelled scrumptious. She wanted him with a desire that bordered on obsession.

"They're packed away with my winter clothes."

Lowering his head, Ivan kissed her icy fingertips. "I think it's time you unpacked your winter clothes. Don't you know you could get frostbite?"

Nayo sucked her teeth. "Now who is being dramatic? I grew up in a little town near the Adirondack Mountains where we had two seasons—summer and winter."

"I thought I heard an upstate inflection in your speech."

Her eyes narrowed. "Do you have something against upstate folks?"

"Not in the least. In fact, I find them more laid-back than people from downstate."

Nayo tried extricating her hands, but she was no match for Ivan's strength. "I never knew what 'flipping the bird' meant until I came here to go to school."

Ivan smiled. "Have you ever given someone the finger?"

Her smile matched his. "Yes. In fact, I did the other day when a cab driver came within inches of hitting me. Not only did he get the finger but also a few choice four-letter words."

"No!" Ivan's expression registered shock.

"Oh, hell, yeah," she drawled, rolling her head on her neck. "You're going to have to let go of my hands so I can give you dessert before it melts."

"What did you bring?" he asked, releasing her hands.

Reaching into the tote, she took out a plastic container. "It's homemade pistachio gelato."

Ivan took the container. "Who made it?"

"I did."

With wide eyes, he stared at her, then the container of frozen dessert. "You make gelato?"

Nayo rolled her eyes. "Yes, Ivan. Now please put it in the freezer before it gets too soft."

Standing at attention, Ivan saluted her. "Yes, ma'am, sir."

"Which one am I?" Nayo asked, smiling.

His gaze moved slowly over her face, down to her chest and still lower to her hips. A black sweater and matching jeans could not disguise the curves that made for a lush, compact body. He smiled at seeing her tiny feet in a pair of thick, black socks.

"You're definitely a ma'am."

Nayo wanted to tell Ivan she wasn't old enough to be a ma'am, but the words were locked in the back of her throat. The way he was looking at her warmed her blood until she found difficulty in drawing a normal breath.

Her eyelids fluttered wildly. "Don't look at me like that."

"Like what, Nayo?" Ivan asked in a voice that was barely above a whisper.

"Like…like…"

"Like I'm the big bad wolf bent on eating the sweet little maiden?"

"Something like that," she mumbled under her breath.

Reaching for her hand, Ivan pulled her along with him as he made his way to the kitchen. "Don't worry, Nayo. I won't take a nibble unless you give me permission."

What was there about her that gave off the vibes that told men she was available for their sexual amusement? Geoff had been forthcoming when he admitted he wanted more than friendship, that he wanted to sleep with her. They'd sleep together, then what?

She'd never been one to engage in gratuitous sex. It hadn't happened when she was twenty and now that she was in her thirties she'd become even more discriminating. Not only were there STDs that couldn't be cured by penicillin, but she'd heard stories from women who'd invited strange men home with them and were lucky to have survived the ordeal with their lives.

She'd thought her parents were just talking out of the side of their necks when they warned her about the dangers of moving to the big city. It'd only taken a single incident for Nayo to acknowledge their warnings bore truth. She'd arranged to meet a fellow photography major to work on a joint project, and as soon as she'd walked through the door of his apartment, he'd pounced on her like a large cat. A well-aimed knee to his groin had disabled him long enough for her to escape. When she'd seen him again in class, he'd acted as if nothing had happened. It was only when Nayo had gotten in his face that he apologized, saying he'd had too much to drink. Drunk or not, she'd threatened to have him arrested for attempted rape if he even looked her way again.

They'd spent the next four years avoiding each other, and on the day of graduation he'd given her a gift with a note saying he'd enrolled in AA after the incident and had been sober ever since. When she'd returned to her Village apartment and opened the exquisitely wrapped box, she'd received the shock of her life. He'd given her a brand-new Nikon camera with a set of lenses that had cost a small fortune. Nayo had never gotten to thank him for the gift because he'd left the state to return to Wisconsin.

She owned several cameras, including the twelve-point, three-megapixel Nikon D90, the revolutionary digital camera with D-SLR. It had the capability of capturing high-definition movie clips that enabled her to use interchangeable lenses for video, as well as stills. The most amazing feature of the camera was its incredible shutter speed of four-point-five frames a second.

However, her first Nikon had become a sentimental favorite and she'd used it to shoot many of the bridges. The photographs in which she'd wanted to capture time-lapse changes in light, she used the D90.

Ivan let go of Nayo's hand when he opened the freezer to store the gelato. "Coffee, tea or cocoa," he asked when he turned to look at her standing in the middle of the kitchen. He didn't know why, but she appeared so small, delicate.

"I'll take cocoa, but only if you have marshmallows."

Reaching for a pot hanging from a hook on the overhead rack, Ivan gave her a warm smile. "You're in luck. My niece came to visit last weekend and she'll only drink cocoa if it has cream or marshmallows."

Nayo moved closer to the stove top when Ivan opened a cabinet for a jar of cocoa powder and another jar filled with tiny marshmallows. He walked back to the refrigerator to get a bottle of milk. She went over and took the milk from him.

"How old is your niece?"

"She's nine going on ninety. I'm constantly reminding my sister that she gave birth to an old soul."

"I'm surprised you would say that."

"Say what?"

"Talk about people having old souls. You're a psychologist, and as a scientist, don't you only believe in what can be proved with empirical evidence?" Nayo watched Ivan pour milk into the pot, then turn on a burner in the induction-cooker stove top. She found it odd to cook without a visible flame.

Ivan gave Nayo a sidelong glance as he poured cocoa into the milk, stirring it with a wooden spoon. "There are some things that will always remain a mystery to science. Despite all the advances in modern medicine, doctors still don't know what triggers the onset of labor in a pregnant woman."

"'Render unto Caesar what belongs to Caesar and unto God all that belongs to Him.'"

"Well said." Ivan grinned.

Ivan removed the pot from the burner before it bubbled over. Reaching out, he caught Nayo around the waist, lifting her effortlessly above his head. She screamed as he straightened his arms and held her aloft as if she were a small child.

He lowered his arms and tossed her up like a beach ball, catching her against his chest. Nayo screamed again and Ivan felt the air on the back of his neck stand up. When he saw her face, he recognized fear in her eyes.

"I'm sorry, baby," he murmured, placing soft kisses on her hair and forehead.

Within seconds sheer panic was replaced by a blinding rage, and Nayo drew back her fist and punched Ivan's chest. "Ouch!" Her hand had landed against solid muscle.

"You can hit me again if it will make you feel better."

"Yeah, so I can break my hand."

Bending slightly, Ivan lowered Nayo until her sock-covered feet touched the tiles on the kitchen floor. "I'm sorry I frightened you."

She narrowed her eyes at him. "You have enough weights downstairs, so there's no excuse to use me for a barbell."

"I said I was sorry. Don't you believe me?" he asked when she continued to glare at him. He took a step. "Maybe you need a little convincing."

Nayo didn't have time to react when she found herself cradled against the solid hardness of Ivan's chest as his head came down. She opened her mouth to protest, but anything she was going to say was cut off when his mouth covered hers in a kiss that sucked the air from her lungs.

The mouth she'd stared at, remembered in her sleep, wanted to photograph, silently coaxed her into responding even when she hadn't wanted to. The arms wrapped around her body felt like bands of steel, and when Nayo swallowed the moist warmth of Ivan Campbell's breath, she knew she was fighting a losing battle.

Her body went pliant as she gave in to the warming glow that began between her legs and spread up and outward, reaching her extremities. Ivan had warned of frostbite when he should've warned her that his kisses had the power to heat her blood to boiling. Curving her arms under his shoulders, she held on to him as waves of passion buffeted her like a tiny boat in a storm.

"Ivan!" It took Nayo a few seconds to recognize her own voice. It'd dropped an octave. "Please let me go," she whispered against his soft, firm lips.

Ivan blinked as if coming out of a trance. He wasn't certain what prompted him to kiss Nayo, but he had no intention of apologizing. For frightening her, yes; kissing her, no.

"Go and sit in front the fire, sweetheart. I'll bring your cocoa."

Nayo nodded numbly. Walking on shaking legs, she moved trancelike out of the kitchen to the alcove. Her heart was still beating a runaway rhythm when she collapsed on a leather chair with a matching footstool.

How did he know?

How did Ivan know she'd wanted him to kiss her?

If she were truly honest with herself, then she would've told him that she wanted more than a kiss.

This was only the third time she'd been with Ivan Campbell, and she wanted him to make love to her.

Chapter 5

Ivan saw Nayo watching him as he approached her with the two mugs of cocoa. He handed her a mug and set his down on a side table. Walking over to the fireplace, he added a piece of wood to the grate, waited for it to catch fire before replacing the screen.

Ivan sat on the sofa and picked up his mug. "How is it?"

"Delicious."

"Are you warm enough?"

"Yes, thanks."

"Let me know when you want to eat and I'll call in an order."

Nayo continued to stare at Ivan as she tried to sort out why she'd felt so drawn to him when it hadn't been that way with other men. Her gaze lingered on his powerful legs in the walking shorts. She hid a smile behind the mug. His feet were as perfect as his hands.

A silence descended and Nayo felt a gentle calm easing into her like a silent fog blanketing the ground. The only other time she'd felt like this was when she'd sat studying a subject through the lens of her camera. Everything else ceased to exist except what she saw in the tiny viewfinder.

Her fingers tightened around the mug, wishing it was a camera so she could capture the image of the man sitting a few feet away. The lighting was subdued, the flickering flames in the fireplace casting long and short shadows on the pale walls. There was only the popping sound from the burning wood competing with the steady tapping of sleet against the windows. She drew in a breath, then let it out slowly.

"What are you thinking about, Nayo?" Ivan's soothing voice floated across the space separating them.

She set down her mug on a glass coaster. "I was thinking how much I wished I had my camera right now."

One of his eyebrows rose. "And what would you do with it?"

"Shoot you."

Ivan smiled, the sensual gesture never failing to

make her stomach flip-flop. "You're serious, aren't you, about wanting to photograph me."

Nayo sat up straighter. "I've never been more serious in my life."

"What made you decide to become a photographer?"

She successfully concealed her disappointment with a too-bright smile. "My grandmother gave me a camera for my tenth birthday and I went around snapping pictures of everything—birds, flowers, cats, dogs and my classmates whenever they weren't looking. By the time I got to high school and became a photographer for the school newspaper, I knew I'd found my passion.

"My parents were upset because they believed I'd never make a living taking pictures, but it was my grandmother who encouraged me to follow my dream. She used her life savings to underwrite the cost of my trip across the country. Unfortunately she passed away soon after I returned home. Everything I've achieved I owe to her."

"How many exhibits have you had?"

"Last week's was my first one."

"It looked as if it was a rousing success."

"It was," Nayo confirmed. When Geoff called to tell her how much her pictures sold for, she was astounded at the amount.

"Congratulations. Now you're a professional photographer."

"It was my first showing, but not the first time I've

sold my work. I've photographed several weddings and a sweet sixteen."

"How do you get your commissions?"

"They're usually by referral."

Nayo took a surreptitious glance at her watch. It was nearly four o'clock. She'd been prepared to go to work, but a call from her boss at the auction house that the heating system wasn't working had given her an unexpected day off. She'd taken advantage of the extra time to shop, clean her apartment and pick up her laundry. A subsequent call from Geoff that a friend of his was hosting a pre-Halloween party rounded out her week. Geoff told her she could invite anyone she wanted and the party was to be held in a TriBeCa loft.

Ivan pushed to his feet. "I guess you're ready to show me the photos."

Nayo managed to look sheepish. "Was I that obvious?"

"You were looking at your watch."

"I just don't want to take up too much of your time."

Ivan closed the distance between them, extending his hand and easing Nayo to her feet. "For you, I will always make time. And yes," he said when she opened her mouth, "I will let you photograph me."

Nayo launched herself at Ivan, her arms going around his neck. "Thank you," she chanted over and over between the kisses she planted on his lean jaw. "I'll pay you."

"No. Whatever you intend to pay me you can send to my favorite charity."

"What's your favorite charity?"

"Gerry Clubhouse. It's under the auspices of The Boys' Club of New York." It was at the East Harlem facility that he'd learned to swim, play chess and box. Reaching up, Ivan pulled her arms down and took a step backward. He didn't want Nayo to know that her spontaneity had aroused him to the point he had an erection. "You can thank me later."

She froze. "How, Ivan?"

"If you're not doing anything, I'd like for you to go out with me Saturday night."

"I'll go out with you Saturday if you go to the Halloween party with me on Friday."

Ivan flashed the smile she'd come to look for. "Okay. But I'm not wearing a costume."

Nayo made a moue. "I think you could be a very dashing Robin Hood."

"I can't imagine myself in tights. And what would you go as? Maid Marian?"

"I don't think so. I'm too short to wear a long dress. I'd rather go as a backup-video dancer and shake my booty."

"I don't think so, Nayo. I don't want to get arrested for thumping some dude ogling you."

"It would never come to that because most the dudes will probably be ogling you."

"Oh-kay," Ivan drawled. "It's *that* type of party."

"There will be something for everyone there."

"Whatever," he drawled again. Ivan never viewed someone's sexual orientation as a problem unless it was a gender-identity disorder.

"I suggest we start looking at the contact sheets before it gets too late. I'm going to have to use your computer because I've transferred all the prints to disks."

Nayo sat next to Ivan in his home office, scrolling through the many photos she'd taken but had decided not to exhibit until her next showing. An all-news radio station played in the background. An updated weather forecast captured her complete attention, and she and Ivan exchanged a knowing glance. An ice storm was blanketing the five boroughs, and the mayor had issued a city-wide alert that all non-emergency vehicles were to stay off street and roads.

Ivan got up and turned on a flat-screen television sitting on its own stand on a shelf of built-in bookcases. WEATHER EMERGENCY flashed across the screen in large red letters while a crawl at the bottom of the screen told of closings and accidents. There was footage of pedestrians attempting to navigate ice-encrusted streets and sidewalks, many of them slipping and falling.

"I suppose there's not going to be any food deliveries tonight," he muttered under his breath.

Nayo, rising to her feet, joined him in front of the

television. "I'm going to leave you with the disks so you can look them over."

He glared down at her. "Where are you going?"

"I'm leaving to go home before I won't be able to get there."

Ivan stared at Nayo as if she'd spoken a foreign language. "You're not going anywhere in this weather. Did you hear the mayor caution people about staying off the streets? And that means pedestrians."

"I can't stay here!"

"Yes, you can, Nayo. I do have more than one bedroom. I'll give you something to sleep in and whatever toiletries you'll need."

Nayo didn't want to believe she would have to spend the night under the roof of a man who made her feel things she didn't want to feel, a man who made her want to do things that she didn't need to do.

What she didn't want to think about was if the scenario had been reversed. If they'd met in her apartment, Ivan would've been forced to spend the night with her. She would've offered him her bed while she'd've slept on the convertible sofa.

"Oh!" she gasped when seeing a woman go down hard on the sidewalk outside the television studios at Times Square. "I suppose you've got yourself a houseguest."

"Why, Nayo," he crooned, "does it sound as if you've just been given a death sentence? I'm not a rapist or Jack the Ripper."

"When we agreed to get together, I hadn't expected a sleepover."

Ivan wrapped an arm around her waist. "Neither had I. But if we'd planned for a sleepover, I would've made other preparations."

A slight frown creased Nayo's smooth forehead. "What are you talking about?"

"I would've asked you what you wanted and if within reason, I would make it happen."

"Are you usually so accommodating?"

"If it's someone I like, yes."

"You like me?"

A beat passed. "Yes. I like you a lot, Nayo."

"Why?"

Another beat passed as Ivan stared at the woman staring up at him, wondering if she was flattered by his interest in her. He'd tried not coming on too hard or quickly because he didn't want to scare her away. Usually he waited for women to approach him, because he didn't like rejection. The first and only woman to whom he'd openly admitted loving had laughed in his face.

However, it was different with Nayo Goddard. He'd come to her showing, engaged in dialogue about her work, and to continue the exchange, agreed to see her again.

"I don't know," Ivan answered truthfully.

"You don't know and I don't know why I'm entertaining your advances."

"Perhaps you like me, too."

"Perhaps," Nayo countered noncommittally.

She had no intention of admitting that she did like him, perhaps a little too much, after just a third encounter. What she feared was that her attraction to Ivan Campbell was based on a physical need. It'd been a while since she'd slept with a man, and there was something about Ivan, a sexual magnetism he projected, she couldn't ignore.

Dipping his head, Ivan pressed his mouth to her ear. "Once we finish with business, we can deal with what it is I like about you."

"You sound very confident that we'll continue to see each other once we conclude *business*."

"You've asked me to go to a party with you on Friday and you've agreed to go out with me Saturday."

"That's only one weekend, Ivan."

He winked at her. "It's a start, beautiful."

Yes, Nayo thought. It was only one weekend and enough time for her to determine whether she wanted to continue to see Ivan after he sat for her. He had most of what a normal woman looked for and expected from a man, but there was a modicum of arrogance in him that nagged at her. Ivan probably would've called it self-confidence, but whatever it was, she couldn't afford to become so absorbed in his attention that it affected her career.

She'd ended her engagement when she overheard

her fiancé tell his brother that he would always be what he considered "piss poor" because his fiancée wanted to run around the world taking pictures, rather than take over her parents' restaurant. When she accused Jerrell Nicholls of using her, he in turn accused her of eavesdropping on a private conversation. It took less than a minute to return his ring and walk out of his life.

Nayo didn't remember much after that because she'd driven around aimlessly for hours before stopping at the small lake where she and Jerrell would go when they wanted to be alone. Six weeks later Nayo left Beaver Run. Upon her return four years later, the town had changed and so had Nayo Cassandra Goddard.

"What was that?" Ivan asked when he heard a strange rumbling sound that hadn't come from the television.

"What are you talking about?" Nayo asked, answering his question with one of her own.

"That rumbling sound?"

Nayo realized where the sound was coming from when it happened again. "I have a confession to make."

Ivan held his breath, praying Nayo wasn't going to tell him that she was involved with someone, or maybe had an estranged husband lurking in her past. He'd never met anyone like this quirky photographer. She was a professional photographer who went by a single name and wore tailored clothes and designer shoes to her showing. Then there was Nayo Goddard, who admitted she'd wanted to become an actress and when dressed casually reminded him of an ingenue with her fresh-scrubbed face and all-black attire.

"What is it?"

"I'm so hungry I could eat half a cow."

Twin emotions of apprehension and relief swept through Ivan. "Why didn't you say something before? I could've either picked up something or called in an order before you got here."

"I usually don't skip meals, but when I found out that I didn't have to go into work today, I did all the chores I normally would do tomorrow. All I had was a cup of coffee this morning."

"And a cup of cocoa," Ivan said, correcting her. Reaching for the remote, he shut off the television. "Come upstairs with me. I'm no Bobby Flay or Chef Jeff, but I'm certain I can fix something that won't give you ptomaine poisoning."

"You do all right with coffee and cocoa."

"There's not much you can do to ruin coffee, but I've been told that I'm sorely lacking in grilling skills."

"Who told you that?"

"Two guys I grew up with."

Nayo glanced at Ivan over her shoulder before she placed her foot on the first stair. "Are they still your friends?"

"I must admit it hurt, but we're tighter than ever."

"That's true friendship, Ivan. A real friend is one

who will tell what you need to know, not what you want to hear."

Ivan stared at the gentle sway of Nayo's hips in the body-hugging jeans as she climbed the staircase. And for the second time in a matter of minutes he felt the stir of arousal. He'd always prided himself on his ability to control his sexual urges, because there had been a time in his life when his libido was so strong he'd diagnosed himself with having hyperactive sexual-desire disorder.

As a high school student he'd gone to bed with girls indiscriminately, until one came to him accusing him of getting her pregnant. Once the initial shock wore off, Ivan realized the possibility of her carrying his child were very slim because he'd always practiced safe sex. No matter how much a woman professed to taking the pill, or was wearing an IUD or, even better, that she couldn't get pregnant, he never deviated from the practice of wearing a condom.

The girl's revelation had shaken him to the core. He, Kyle and Duncan had promised one another they would finish high school, not get hooked on drugs and not father a child out of wedlock. When the girl came back to tell him she'd made a mistake—her cycle was late— Ivan felt as if he'd been given a reprieve. Overactive libido or not, he resorted to other methods to release his sexual frustrations. And once his focus shifted to becoming a psychologist, sleeping with women was no longer a priority. His friends used to tease him because they always saw him with a different woman, but what they didn't know was that he hadn't wanted to get too close to any of them. For him, variety was crucial to achieving his goal.

"Do you have a friend or friends who will always keep it real?" he asked Nayo.

Nayo, walking into the kitchen, turned to face Ivan. "Fortunately I do. I never have to guess what Geoff is thinking. He tells me what is exactly on his mind, whether I want to hear it or not. And most times he's right."

Ivan opened the side-by-side refrigerator/freezer. "I have bacon, eggs, country sausage, orange juice, strawberries and…" His voice trailed off as he peered into the freezer. "I have steak, ground beef, salmon and chicken, but unfortunately they're frozen solid."

"I don't mind breakfast."

"What do you want?"

Nayo joined Ivan. "Do you have pancake mix?"

He nodded. "I think there's a box in the pantry."

"I'll cook."

"Why?"

Nayo smiled. "Because that way I know I won't get ptomaine poisoning," she teased.

Ivan glared at her under lowered lids. "You're looking to get tossed up again."

"You wouldn't, Ivan."

"I would, Nayo."

"Bully," she whispered.

"Yeah, yeah," he countered.

"Are you going to stand there beating your gums, or are you going to assist me?"

"What do you want, Chef Nayo?"

"Do you have any apples?"

Even if Ivan didn't have meat or dairy on hand, his refrigerator was always stocked with fresh fruit. There had been a time when he'd experimented with becoming a vegetarian, but the desire to bite into a piece of meat had been too strong to ignore for long periods of time.

"Yes. Why?"

"What kind?"

"I have several yellow delicious apples and one or two green." His niece had gone apple picking with her fourth-grade class, and when he'd gone to Nyack to visit his sister and her husband, a bag of apples were packed up for him to bring back to Manhattan.

"I need you to peel, core and grate a green apple. Excuse me, Ivan. If you stand there staring at me as if I had a third eye in the middle of my forehead, I'm going to pass out on you. That way you can toss me as many times as you want."

Bowing from the waist, Ivan made a big show of moving away from the refrigerator. "Your wish is my command, princess."

Nayo smiled at his exaggerated theatrics. She took

out the items she needed to put together breakfast, even though the hour indicated dinner would've been more appropriate.

She discovered Ivan's pantry held a treasure trove of canned food, jars of spices and boxes of pasta and a variety of grains. Working quickly and methodically she halved a package of bulk sausage, added the apple Ivan had grated for her, then finely ground bread crumbs, an egg, a couple of tablespoons of heavy cream and sea salt and freshly ground pepper, and fashioned them into patties.

Ivan busied himself setting the table in the expansive eat-in kitchen as the tangy-sweet smell of sausage filled the space. Nayo had cooked the patties on the stove top grill, then transferred them to an ovenproof dish and placed them in the oven's warming drawer.

Ivan loved his mother, but unfortunately he couldn't say the same about her cooking. Winnie Campbell couldn't boil an egg without either under- or overcooking it. If it hadn't been for his grandmother, who lived in a neighboring building, or Kyle's parents he would gone hungry. Kyle's father, Elwin Chatham, who'd been a railroad chef, cooked the most incredible dishes for his family, and whenever Ivan heard that Kyle's father would be home for more than a day or two, he could be found sitting at the Chathams' kitchen table. After a while Frances knew to set a plate for her son's friend whenever her husband was home. When Ivan's future brother-in-law told him he intended to propose marriage to Ivan's sister, his only advice was to give Roberta a gift certificate for cooking lessons. He followed Ivan's advice when he enrolled himself and Roberta in a course for couples who love cooking together.

He crossed the kitchen and stood next to Nayo as she flipped oatmeal-buttermilk pancakes. She'd filled two small bowls with sliced strawberries and chopped walnuts as toppings for the pancakes. "If I make mimosas, will you have one?"

Nayo smiled up at Ivan. "I love mimosas."

She returned her attention to flipping the pancakes, then testing them for doneness before sliding them onto a heated plate. The distinctive pop of a champagne cork echoed in the kitchen. Ivan had turned on a radio to an all-music station, and Nayo found herself singing along with the classic love songs. All she had to do was warm the syrup and she was finished.

Turning off the stove, she carried the platter of pancakes and sausage to the table as Ivan placed two flutes filled with orange juice and topped off with champagne at the place settings. He'd dimmed the lights, but left the ones over the dining area on, creating a soft, romantic look.

Ivan looked sheepish when Nayo bowed her head to say grace. He'd forgotten his home training. Despite not being able to cook well, Winnie wouldn't let anyone pick up a fork without blessing the food.

Picking up his fork, he cut a slice of sausage. He chewed the meat slowly, savoring the distinctive flavor of sage, tart apple and fennel on his tongue. "Oh, damn!" he crooned. "This is incredible. Where did you learn to cook like this?" he asked Nayo, who gazed at him with a mysterious smile softening her mouth.

"My parents own a restaurant."

"*Now* you tell me. I should toss your cute little ass up until you beg me to stop. So why were you trying to trick a brother when you asked if I was going to cook for you?"

"Brothers do cook, Ivan."

He waved a hand. "Didn't you see the cookbooks? That should've told you that *this* brother is a novice. I did admit that I really wasn't that good."

"You do okay," Nayo said as she swallowed a mouthful of mimosa. "You make a wonderful latte, good cocoa and a killer mimosa."

"Man—or should I say mankind—cannot live by drink alone."

"You're probably better than you think. What you need is confidence. Your friends have done you gross disservice. Grilling is one thing and cooking is entirely different. I'm willing to bet that if you had to cook a complete meal for me, it would come out okay."

"You think?"

She smiled. "Yes, I think. Instead of going out to eat on Saturday, why don't you cook dinner for us?"

"Is that what you want?"

"Yes. I prefer home cooking to going out to a restaurant."

"What about your parents' restaurant?"

"It's a family-style restaurant. There's nothing that even remotely resembles gourmet on the menu. If someone wants good pot roast or corned beef hash, they go to the Running Beaver."

Ivan squinted. "Why is it called the Running Beaver?"

"The name of the town is Beaver Run, population 2,383 at the last count."

"So, you're really a small-town girl."

"Yep. Friday-night football, hayrides, apple picking, harvest-moon school dances, swimming in the creek when the weather got too hot and skating on the lake when it froze over."

"And now you're living in the big, bad city."

"It's no worse than living in a small town. The difference is the demographics. Beaver Run does have a police department. We have problems with kids getting hooked on drugs, teenage pregnancy, burglaries and armed robberies. Last year we had the first murder in more than a decade. A kid shot and killed his stepfather because he'd called him stupid in front of his friends. A diss is a diss no matter where it occurs. What do you think of the photos you've seen thus far?" She'd smoothly changed the topic.

Ivan had viewed more than sixty black-and-white photographs, and he'd mentally noted the ones he wanted to hang in his home. Whenever he asked Nayo about a particular shot, she gave him an overview of why she'd decided to capture the image on film.

They talked as they ate, neither seemingly willing to leave the table. Two hours later, they got up to clear the table and clean up the kitchen. They returned to the home office, looking at thumbnail prints Nayo enlarged to fill the computer monitor whenever Ivan expressed an interest in the shot. It was after ten when she walked into the bedroom Ivan had assigned her. He'd given her a T-shirt to sleep in and a plastic bag filled with travel-size toiletries.

"Sleep tight," he said quietly as he crossed the bedroom to the door.

"Don't let the bedbugs bite," came her rejoinder as he closed the door behind his departing figure.

Picking up a remote from the bedside table, she flicked on the television, which sat on a table in the corner of the bedroom. She turned it to the weather channel. Pictures of the freak ice storm that had swept over the Northeast had become the lead story.

She turned off the television and made her way to the adjoining bath. Stripping off her clothes, she placed her sweater and jeans on a chair, then tossed her bra, panties and socks into the shower to wash them. Nayo knew she couldn't ask Ivan to use his washer and dryer for only a pair of silk panties and matching bra and socks. The apartment was warm, and she was certain they would dry in time for her to wear them home tomorrow.

A quarter of an hour later, she climbed into the four-poster, settling the mosquito netting around the bed like a cocoon. Within minutes of her head touching the pillow, she was asleep.

Chapter 6

Ivan closed the case file, then his eyes, wondering why it was so difficult to concentrate. When he'd gotten up earlier that morning, he was surprised to find that the ice coating the sidewalks and roadways had melted with the mid-forty-degree temperature. The steps and the sidewalk in front his brownstone were covered with the sand he'd put down before going to bed. He wasn't willing to risk someone falling and injuring themselves, then suing him.

He'd shaved and showered and gone in search of Nayo, only to find her gone. She'd left a note on the neatly made bed thanking him for his hospitality and hoped they could do it again. Her willingness to have a repeat of the night before countered his disappointment that he hadn't been there to see her leave.

Ivan opened his eyes when he heard three rapid taps on his office door. "Good morning, Kyle."

Kyle Chatham walked into the office and touched fists with Ivan. "You missed the male-bonding session last night."

"Sit down, Kyle."

Waiting until his friend sat, Ivan leaned forward. He'd known Kyle since they were boys, but now that the attorney had proposed marriage to his social-worker girlfriend he appeared more laid-back, less intense. Tall and slender with dark skin that glowed like polished teak, Kyle had one of the brightest legal minds of anyone he'd met.

"What happened last night?" Ivan asked.

"DG and I had to spend the night here. We closed down and sent our staff home as soon as the sleet started freezing, but we weren't that lucky. We didn't make halfway down the block before we were slipping and sliding all over the place. DG wanted to call you and hang out at your place because you only live two blocks away, but I told him you were probably entertaining."

The three offices had executive and staff bathrooms, and Kyle, Duncan and Ivan had left several changes of clothes at the brownstone in the event they had to work around the clock and couldn't get home to change.

"Whether I was or wasn't entertaining, it still wouldn't have made a difference. After all, I did have two available bedrooms."

"Don't you have four bedrooms altogether?"

"You know I do. Come on—ask me if I had company last night."

Kyle bit back a smile. "Did you?"

Ivan ran a hand over his cropped hair. "Yes, I did. But she had her own bedroom."

"Your sister stayed over?"

"No, Kyle. She wasn't my sister."

"Is something up, brother?" Kyle asked.

"Why would you say that?"

"Since when do your women sleep in the guest room?"

"When they're *not* my women. This one came over to discuss business, got stuck, so I put her up for the night." Ivan told Kyle about the design-magazine layout.

"Congratulations, man. You're place is spectacular."

Ivan smiled. "Thank you."

"What's up, brothers?" Kyle and Ivan turned to find Duncan's broad shoulders filling the doorway.

Ivan waved him in. "Come on in, DG."

Duncan, resplendent in a hand-tailored Italian suit, strolled in and sat on the edge of Ivan's desk. The two men touched fists. "Where were you last night?"

"Home."

One silky black eyebrow arched in Duncan's olive-brown face. "Alone?"

Ivan held up both hands. "Yo, brothers. Hold up. What's with the interrogation?"

Duncan shared a knowing look with Kyle. "Kyle and I called your cell and it went directly to voice mail. We thought about calling your house phone but decided you probably were hooked up with your latest honey."

Lacing his fingers together on top of his desk, Ivan gave each of his friends a long, penetrating look. "You guys need to stop trying to micromanage my love life, or lack thereof. You see me with different women and you assume I'm sleeping with them. When, Duncan and Kyle, do I have the time to bed half the women I've seen? You know my caseload, that I teach two classes twice a week, and between hanging out with you guys—no, let me backtrack. I used to hang out with you before we bought this place and you two got engaged. I'm only going to say this once. Back off, and please let me do my thing."

Kyle shook his head. "You're taking it the wrong way, Ivan."

"How should I take it, Kyle?"

Duncan looped one leg over the opposite knee, his eyes narrowing. "What's going on, Ivan? Kyle and I have teased you before and you never came at us like you are now. Why so defensive?"

"When did you become a therapist, DG?"

"Oh, hell, no!" Duncan said between clenched teeth.

Kyle knew Duncan and Ivan were about to butt heads. "Yo, brothers. Cool it. We've been through too much to argue about a woman. Since when have we ever let a woman come between us?"

"Never," they chorused.

"Dr. Campbell— Oops, I didn't know you had company."

Ivan glanced at the clock on the credenza before beckoning his secretary. It was eight-thirty and she was half an hour early. "After you put your things away, I need to see you."

Chantal Howard smiled and nodded to the other men in her boss's office. "Good morning, Mr. Gilmore."

Duncan gave her a warm smile. "Good morning, Chantal."

"Good morning, Mr. Chatham."

Kyle winked at her. Chantal, Duncan's executive assistant and the receptionists had taken turns coming to his second-floor office with the hope of catching a glimpse of Jordan Wainwright, who'd joined Kyle's practice and now was partner. Jordan had become such a distraction that Kyle's office manager had put a stop to their unannounced visits. Jordan, embarrassed by all the attention he was receiving, had elected to take his lunch outside the building rather than eat in the employee dining room.

"Good morning, Chantal. How is Kassim?"

"He's real good, Mr. Chatham. Thanks for asking." She turned to head for her desk.

Duncan lowered his leg. "I know you're expecting a client, Kyle, but I want to get together sometime next weekend. Why don't we hook up Sunday afternoon?"

"Count me in," Kyle said. "I don't mind you guys hanging out at my place. Are you in, Ivan?"

"Yeah, I'm in." Ivan had to ask Nayo if she wanted to go with him to meet his friends. "I told you I want to throw a little something to celebrate your engagement to Tamara," Ivan said to Duncan.

"Are you cooking?" Kyle teased with a wide grin.

Ivan narrowed his gaze. "Matter-of-fact, I am. Now, what are you going to say to that?"

"Are you really cooking?" Duncan asked.

Ivan was saved from answering when Chantal returned. He stood up. "Gentlemen, I'll talk to you later." Kyle and Duncan rose and walked out of the office, muttering about having to eat his cooking.

It would serve them right if he did attempt to prepare the foods for the small, intimate gathering. Duncan, an only child, had only one known relative. He never knew his father, and his mother passed away the year he celebrated his fourteenth birthday. Duncan went to live with his schoolteacher aunt in Brooklyn, but never lost touch with his two best friends from the projects.

He motioned to the chair beside his desk. "Please sit down, Chantal."

Chantal sat, staring at the man who'd hired her when no one would after she'd had Kassim. The moment she mentioned she had a small child, most employers told her they would have to get back to her. And that meant thanks, but no thanks, regardless of her secretarial skills.

She knew by his expression that what Dr. Campbell wanted to talk about did not bode well for her. He was the most generous boss she'd ever had, but she wasn't certain how much longer he would be her boss. A notation on her last evaluation indicated that if she didn't improve her attendance and tardiness, she was in jeopardy of losing her job.

When her mother had come to the office to give her a set of keys, she'd introduced her to Dr. Campbell. Later her mother told her that she should've waited for a man like her boss, rather than take up with the unemployed man who'd gotten her pregnant. Chantal stared at her boss's yellow silk tie. During the months of June, July and August, the psychologist was rarely seen wearing a suit and tie. His colorful Hawaiian shirts, lightweight slacks and slip-ons had become his trademark, warm-weather look.

Ivan gave the young woman a direct stare. "Chantal, I know we've had this conversation before and I'd hoped we wouldn't have to revisit the problem of your lateness and attendance."

Chantal dropped her head. "I'm sorry, Dr. Campbell." A profusion of neatly braided hair fell around her thin face. "I'm having a problem with my son's father—

Big Kassim. He goes out at night after I come home, but doesn't get back in time to take care of Kassim when I have to leave in the morning."

"Is he aware of the time you need to leave to get to work on time?"

"Yes. Most times I have to blow up his cell for him to call me back. Then we get into it because he feels I'm clocking him. I've warned him that I'm going to kick him out, but he says he wants a relationship with his son."

Ivan went completely still. He hadn't known the man was living with Chantal. A muscle in his jaw throbbed noticeably when he clenched his teeth. "Does Big Kassim have a night job?"

Chantal's head came up. "No."

Counting slowly to ten to keep from losing his temper, Ivan's frown deepened. "Where does he go if he's not working?"

The young woman twisted her mouth in a nervous gesture. "I asked him once and he told me he's just hanging out."

"He hangs out every night?"

"Just about."

Ivan wanted to shake Chantal until she was breathless. Talk about denial. It was obvious the man was using her under the guise of wanting a relationship with his son. And if he was hanging out, most likely it was with another woman.

"Well, his hanging out at night has to stop, because I'm not going to put up with you coming in late and taking off because your baby's daddy can't find his way home in time for you to leave for work. I have the name, address and telephone number of the director of a day-care center that's only a few blocks from here." Opening a drawer in his desk, he took out a business card and handed it to Chantal. "I want you to call her and set up an appointment to enroll Kassim in a setting where he can be socialized with other children his age. You have exactly one week to make it happen. That will be all."

Chantal knew she'd been summarily dismissed. What she didn't want was to lose her job. It paid well and had afforded her a modicum of independence when she'd moved out of her mother's apartment into her own place. It wasn't furnished the way she'd wanted it to be, since she'd had to give Big Kassim money because he couldn't find a job.

Rising to her feet on trembling legs, she stared at her boss. "Dr. Campbell, do you think Big Kassim is fooling around with another woman?"

Leaning back in his chair, Ivan gave her an incredulous stare. "You don't want me to answer that."

"Why not?"

"Because you don't want to hear my answer."

"My mother said he's using me."

"I think you should listen to your mother."

"How do I get rid of him, Dr. Campbell?"

"Sit down, Chantal," he ordered in a quiet voice. "I'm not your therapist, but if you were my sister, I'd advise you to give Big Kassim an ultimatum. Either he gets a job or he's out. You can't afford to take care of yourself, your son and a grown-ass, able-bodied man. Even if he gets a position flipping burgers or frying chicken, at least he would earn enough to take care of some of his needs.

"You may not realize it, but you've got two children—your son and your son's father. You're providing shelter, food and clothing—"

"And don't forget the cable premium channels because he wants to watch all the baseball and basketball games," she interrupted angrily.

A grim smile replaced Ivan's scowl. "There you go."

"I can't even save enough money to buy a dinette set because he's always asking me if I have some spare change. Then he complains about eating off TV trays."

Ivan wanted to give the woman a high five. He'd always lectured his patients, the women in particular, to empower themselves, and it was apparent Chantal had finally opened her eyes enough to rid herself of the leech sucking her dry.

"I think you know what you should do. I need you to give me the case files for today's patients. Then call the day-care center and get your son into a safe, healthy social environment."

Chantal popped up like a jack-in-the-box. "Thank you, Dr. Campbell."

Pushing back his chair, he stood. "You're welcome, Chantal."

Ivan was still standing when Chantal left his office, closing the door behind her. His first patient was an Iraqi war veteran with multiple deployments who'd been diagnosed with PTSD, post-traumatic stress disorder. He'd been referred to a psychiatrist at a local veterans' hospital, but he claimed he didn't like the doctor because he'd prescribed medication that made him feel like a zombie.

U.S. Army Corporal Billie Shannon had been scheduled for a dishonorable discharge after attacking his superior officer before he was reevaluated and granted a medical discharge, after a psychiatric evaluation ruled he exhibited all the signs associated with PTSD. Soldiers who were granted medical discharges were entitled to veteran benefits.

Retaking his seat, Ivan opened the file again to review the notes from the last session. Five minutes before Billie was scheduled, he turned off the overhead light, switched on a table lamp and adjusted the window blinds, shutting out most of the sunlight and creating a soft, calming environment.

Within seconds of Chantal's escorting the former soldier into the office, Ivan felt the man's agitation. But after spending a wonderful night with Nayo, he was prepared for whatever the day presented.

* * *

"Nayo, please come look at this."

"What is it, Dyana?" She continued to stuff large, square, white envelopes with the catalogs she'd spent months designing for the small auction house. Ryker's wasn't as well-known as Christie's or Sotheby's, but their list of elite clients was a testament to their success.

"I need your help identifying the figure on this dish cover."

Smothering a curse, Nayo walked over to a work-table where Dyana Ryker sat with several hand-painted plates cradled in bubble wrap. She wanted to finish stuffing the envelopes, put them in the mail before the five-o'clock pickup, then go home to relax before preparing for the pre-Halloween party later that evening. She'd sent Ivan a text, giving him her address and the time he should pick her up. The text also included the address of the loft where the party was to be held. He'd returned her text, typing he looked forward to see her again.

Peering over the shoulder of the auction-house owner, Nayo studied the figure of a cherub perched on the outer edge of a dish cover. "That's a *putto*. It's Italian for 'boy' or 'cherub.'"

Dyana stared at Nayo over a pair of rimless half-glasses. "Isn't it a little strange to find an Italian ornament on a nineteenth-century Copenhagen dish cover?"

"Angelic spirits were used during the Renaissance

and were still very popular in the Baroque period. This piece is an example of Renaissance Revival and probably a holdover from the seventeenth century."

"We have only four pieces in this set. I really don't see how we're going to sell it."

Nayo returned to the task of stuffing envelopes. She didn't want to engage in a dialogue with the long-winded Dyana, because she'd never leave. The woman had earned the reputation as one of the most knowledgeable collectors of antiques. Tall, thin and anemic-looking in appearance, she could recognize ceramics from ancient China to twentieth-century toys with a cursory glance.

The Upper East Side shop was not much more than a junk shop, where Andres Ryker, Dyana's now-deceased husband, had paid little or nothing to those who didn't know the value of an heirloom. When Dyana had walked into the shop and offered to pay Andres ten times the sticker price for a French opaline scent bottle, circa 1845, Andres asked the young art-history student to come work for him. He hired Dyana and married her a year later. After forty years of a loving, childless marriage he died, leaving Dyana bereft but incredibly wealthy. There was never a time Nayo saw Dyana wear any color other than black. And with her flaxen hair pulled tightly off her pale face, blue eyes and somber attire, she reminded Nayo of a vampire.

"Someone will eventually purchase it," she said.

Dyana's pale lips parted in a smile. "They always do. I've decided not to open Monday."

Nayo removed the strips on the flaps of the self-sealing envelopes before affixing postage to the stack with domestic addresses. "What's happening Monday?"

"It's that dreadful day where people believe it's okay to run amok. One year a group of children came into the shop and broke a Lalique dish. I made a solemn promise to Andres and myself that I would never open on Halloween."

"Do you want me to come in on Tuesday to make up for Monday?"

"No, Nayo. We're a little slow right now, so you can come in on Wednesday as scheduled."

Nayo enjoyed working for Dyana because regardless of whether she worked one day or three, she was still paid her full salary. Dyana had hinted that she wanted her to come onboard full-time, but Nayo needed at least two days off each week for her photography.

The only exception was when Dyana took on the job of estate liquidator. They usually spent weeks, sometimes months, identifying and pricing antique items.

She finished the envelopes in time to put them into a mailbox on the corner before the mail carrier came to empty the box. Returning to the shop, she gathered up her tote. "How long are you staying before you lock up?" she asked Dyana.

"I plan to be out of here by six."

"Have a good weekend. I'll see you Wednesday."

Dyana smiled. "You enjoy your weekend."

I plan to, Nayo mused as she walked to the door. "Thank you," she said, instead.

She knew Dyana would probably remain here much later than six. She didn't have far to go home—she lived in an apartment above the shop. Not only did she own the spacious, six-room apartment, but also the entire four-story building.

Nayo always took the bus uptown rather than the subway because she preferred sitting down to standing up. It took her longer to get home, but at least she wasn't jostled or sandwiched between people who didn't care what they ate or drank before blowing their fetid breath in her face.

It was completely dark by the time she turned down her block. The clocks were scheduled to go back an hour this coming weekend, and that meant she would gain an extra hour of sleep, but it also meant fewer hours of natural daylight—light she needed when photographing her subjects. She'd told Ivan to pick her up at eight-thirty. The party was scheduled to begin at eight, and by the time they arrived around nine it would be in full swing.

She didn't see Mrs. Anderson or Colin when she got to her floor, but heard canned laughter from a sitcom through the door of her neighbor's apartment. There were times the volume on the television was turned up so loud Nayo suspected the woman had a hearing problem.

Tossing her mail and magazines on the table with her computer, she slipped out of her shoes and coat. She checked her phone. The display read: No MISSED CALLS. She had nothing to distract her as she prepared for her date.

Date. The word sounded strange because she couldn't remember the last time she'd actually had a date. She didn't count the times she went to a movie, a restaurant or a party with Geoff as dates. He was her friend and she was his friend. Holding hands or a slight brush of their lips was the extent of their physical contact. People usually gave them a second look when they walked down the street together, not because they appeared to be an interracial couple but because they were complete opposites. Geoff was tall and blond and she was short and dark. Whenever she went out with him, she tended to wear heels in an attempt to minimize the height difference. She was five-two in her bare feet and Geoff six-two.

Most of her friends had become Geoff's friends and vice versa. They were a cohesive group of about twenty, many of whom were artists or involved in the arts. The woman hosting tonight's party was a professional dancer who'd set up a dance studio in her TriBeCa loft.

Using the remote, Nayo turned on the television to catch the evening news. The temperature was forty-two with clear skies. She smiled. At least they wouldn't have to put up with rain or sleet. Stripping off her clothes, she walked on bare feet to the bathroom. She'd planned to take a leisurely bath, but now decided to take a shower and wash her hair. An electric curling brush usually worked wonders with her short hair.

Nayo wielded the curling brush like a professional as she dried her hair. The normally tight curls were looser, making it appear as if her hair had miraculously grown several inches. Using her fingers, she picked at the hair on the crown to give the illusion of added height. Satisfied with the results, she left the bathroom and walked over to her bed to get dressed.

She'd wear the ubiquitous New York City black: a body-hugging, jersey dress with long sleeves, a mock turtleneck and a hem at her knees, along with sheer black hose. A pair of black suede pumps added three inches to her diminutive height.

Nayo had just returned to the bathroom to apply her makeup when the intercom buzzed. She glanced at the glowing numbers on the clock-radio on a shelf in the bathroom. It was only minutes after eight. The intercom buzzed again. She wondered if it was someone who lived in the building who had forgotten their keys.

Walking over to the panel on the wall, she pressed the talk button. "Yes?"

"It's Ivan."

Her knees buckled slightly before she recovered. He was early. Too early. She'd told him to pick her up downstairs at eight-thirty. Knowing she couldn't leave him waiting until she finished getting dressed, she pressed the button, disengaging the door that led to the street.

Nayo managed to put away her bathrobe and slippers before she heard the soft knock on her door. Glancing around, she took a deep breath. Ivan Campbell would be the first man, aside from her brother and father, to cross her threshold.

A polite smile was in place when she opened the door. She took another breath. Ivan was so breathtakingly virile dressed completely in black that she was momentarily stunned. A V-neck sweater displayed his brown throat, and his cashmere jacket with its European cut was draped over his broad shoulders before tapering slightly at the waist. She recognized the fabric of his slacks as flannel.

Nayo opened the door wider. "Please come in. I'll be ready as soon as I finish with my makeup."

Ivan couldn't pull his gaze away from Nayo's face and body. The dress clung to every curve of her body. Nayo Goddard was sexy personified in one neat little package. His gaze moved down to her legs and feet. How had he forgotten those legs?

"I'm here early because my driver showed up earlier than I'd expected."

"You hired a driver?"

Ivan smiled. "Yes. I own a car, but I rarely drive in the city because I can never find parking."

"We could have taken a cab."

His gaze caressed her flawless face. "I don't take taxis." The one time he'd tried to, he'd stood in the rain watching taxi after taxi pass him by because he was standing on the uptown side of the street. Angry and exasperated after twenty minutes, he took the subway back to Harlem. That was three years ago, and his vow not to take another New York City taxi was still in effect.

"You always use a car service to get around the city?"

"Most of the time I do. But that doesn't mean I won't hop on a bus or take the subway if I'm going a short distance."

"Come talk to me while I put on makeup." Turning, she walked to the bathroom, Ivan following.

His gaze lingered on the four-poster bed draped in embroidered mosquito netting. "I like your apartment."

"Thank you. When my brother came for a visit with his son, my nephew wanted to know why I sleep in the same space as my kitchen. Even after I explained to him that this is what is called a studio apartment, he still couldn't understand that if the bathroom had a door, why couldn't the kitchen."

Leaning against the door frame, Ivan watched Nayo apply makeup so subtly it appeared she was wearing nothing. Brushes and tiny pots of color accentuated her eyes, cheeks and lips. She ran a wide-tooth comb through her hair, adding height and volume. He straightened when she washed, then dried her hands. The sensual scent of her perfume wafted to his nostrils as she came closer.

Nayo tried getting around Ivan, but there wasn't enough room—he blocked the doorway. "Ivan."

Not moving, he stared at her under hooded lids. "Yes, Nayo?"

"You're going to have to move."

"What if I don't want to move?"

She closed her eyes. "Then we won't go to the party."

"Is that such a bad thing, doll face?" Her eyes opened. "We could spend the night here."

"No, Ivan. We will not spend the night here. Either we leave and go to the party or I'm going without you."

"You'd leave me here alone?"

"Yes, I would. You can lounge on the bed, watch television or raid the refrigerator. The choice is yours."

The seconds ticked by as they stared at each other. "I choose to go to the party with you," Ivan said after an interminable pause.

"That's what I thought."

"You don't have to sound so smug."

Nayo winked at Ivan as he stepped aside. She went to the closet and took out a black, three-quarter-length mohair coat. Ivan was beside her, taking the coat. He held it as she slipped her arms into the sleeves. Gathering her keys and a tiny leather purse with a shoulder strap, she turned off the track lights, leaving on a floor lamp.

She locked the door and Ivan took the keys from her hand. "I'll hold on to them."

He descended the staircase, Nayo following closely behind. His arm went around her waist when they stepped onto the sidewalk. "The driver is parked around the corner on Madison."

Robert was out of the car and waiting as they approached. He opened the rear door. "Good evening, miss."

Nayo gave him a warm smile. "Good evening to you, too."

She slipped onto the leather seat, moving over as Ivan got in beside her. In a moment of madness she'd tried imagining herself married to Ivan Campbell. Why, she chided herself, was she indulging in flights of fantasy? For that was exactly what it was—pure fantasy. Leaning against his shoulder, she sank into the comfort of his warmth and strength. She closed her eyes when he pressed his face against her hair.

"You smell good enough to eat," Ivan whispered.

A shiver raced through Nayo's body. How did he know she was thinking the same thoughts? From the moment she first saw him, she knew there was something very different about the man in whose arms she now lay, and it had nothing to do with his face.

It was the man, one she'd found herself fantasizing about when she least expected. Unknowingly Dr. Ivan Campbell had become her fantasy man.

Chapter 7

Brooke Simons had spared no expense for the Halloween party in her loft. Someone was on hand to check coats, and a waitstaff circulated among the guests offering hot and cold hors d'oeuvres. A bar, set up against a wall, was doing a brisk business, while a DJ played nonstop music that had most up on their feet dancing. Only a few partygoers had chosen to come in costume.

Nayo, her arm wrapped around Ivan's waist, introduced him to their hostess. "Brooke, this is my good friend Ivan Campbell. Ivan, this is Brooke Simons."

Brooke's large dark eyes widened appreciably

when she smiled at Ivan. She offered her hand. "My pleasure, Ivan."

He took her hand, returning her smile. "The pleasure is mine. Your loft is spectacular."

"Thank you. Please circulate and make certain you get something to eat and drink."

Nayo had to agree with Ivan. Brooke had dimmed the recessed lights in the expansive space, and hundreds of flickering votives and tea lights twinkled like stars. A dozen, small round tables, each with seating for four, were set up at the far end of the room.

She spied Geoff as he walked with a beautiful young Asian woman clinging possessively to his arm. When she'd asked him who he was bringing to the party, he told her he hadn't decided.

Geoffrey Magnus was a good catch for the woman who could get him to stand still long enough to propose marriage. His striking good looks, intelligence and family lineage made him one of the city's most eligible bachelors.

"Can I get you something to drink?" Ivan asked quietly.

"I'll have whatever you're having."

His eyebrows shot up. "Are you sure?"

"Very sure."

Nayo smiled at Geoff as he approached, then offered her cheek for his kiss. "How are you?"

His gray eyes softened with an unknown emotion. "Wonderful, now that I've seen you."

A slight frown marred her smooth forehead. Geoff had come to the party with another woman, yet he was coming on to her. She extended her hand to the tall, waif-thin woman with the dark, smoky eye makeup and curtain of straight black hair ending at her waist. "I'm Nayo."

"Michiko," came her throaty reply. "You're the photographer."

"Yes."

Michiko smiled up at Geoff. "Geoffrey showed me some of your work and I told him I want you to take photos of me for my portfolio."

"You're a model."

Michiko nodded. "Yes. I was told by the booker at an agency that she could book me for a few jobs, but I need a more professional portfolio."

"You want me to do your portfolio." The question came out like a statement.

"Yes."

Nayo gave Geoff a sidelong glance. He winked at her. "Geoffrey has my business card. Call me and we'll talk."

"Money is not an issue. I'll pay you whatever you charge."

Nayo wanted to tell the woman photography wasn't only about money. It was satisfaction for the one being photographed and the photographer. Her expression changed when she saw Ivan closing the distance between them, holding a glass with a dark brown liquid in each hand.

Ivan nodded to the tall, blond man and the tall, thin woman talking to Nayo. He handed her one of the glasses. "Here's your drink."

She wrinkled her nose. "It looks like a cola."

Ivan smiled. "But it tastes like a black dog."

"What's in a black dog?"

"Bourbon, dry vermouth and blackberry brandy," Geoff stated confidently as he exchanged a high five with Ivan.

He'd told Nayo he'd become a professional "mixologist," not because he needed to earn money, but to meet women. Those meeting him for the first time did not link him to the celebrated family who bought, sold, collected and loaned art to major museums throughout the country. She'd allowed him exactly sixty seconds to wallow in self-pity, then called him a poor little rich boy and told him to get over it.

"Ivan Campbell," Ivan said, introducing himself. "I like a man who knows his cocktails."

"Geoff Magnus, closet mixologist. And this lovely lady is Michiko."

Michiko wiggled her fingers at Ivan. "Hi."

Nayo did a double take, wondering if she was looking at the same woman. Michiko's contralto had gone up an octave as she licked her lips and batted her lashes at Ivan.

"Excuse me, but Ivan and I are going to get something to eat." Looping her arm through his, Nayo steered Ivan away from the couple.

"What was that all about?" he asked when they were far enough away for Geoff and his date not to overhear them.

"The nerve of that heifer!"

"Who's a heifer?"

"Hi-eee," Nayo said, mimicking the wannabe model.

A knowing smile tilted the corners of Ivan's firm mouth. "Don't tell me you're jealous."

"Hell, yeah, I'm jealous, Ivan. The woman's normal voice is almost as deep as yours."

"That's because we have the same anatomical plumbing. Close your mouth, darling." Her jaw had dropped open.

"No!" Nayo gasped.

Moving closer, he angled his head and brushed a kiss over her mouth. "Yes. And I'm flattered that you're jealous."

Going on tiptoe, Nayo pressed a kiss to the corner of his mouth. "That's because I like you."

Ivan touched his glass to hers. "I'll drink to that." Putting the glass to his mouth, he took a deep swallow. "Nice."

Nayo took a tentative sip, finding the drink much stronger than she was used to. "I think you're trying to get me drunk so you can take advantage of me."

Ivan's expression changed like quicksilver. "I don't want to take advantage of you."

She also sobered. "What *do* you want?"

He leaned closer. "I want to make love to you."

Nayo closed her eyes. How, she wondered, did he know what she wanted, had unconsciously wanted from the moment she saw him at the gallery? It'd begun when he'd shaken her hand and she'd felt a burning awareness, shattering her resolve not to become involved with a man.

When she opened her eyes, it was to Ivan gazing at her with a tender expression she'd never seen before. She had met him exactly one week ago, yet it felt as if she'd known him as long as she had Geoff. With Ivan she could be herself. There was no need to weigh every word that came to mind in the hope he wouldn't be offended.

A hint of a smile parted her lips. "I know."

"You know?"

Ivan wondered if he'd been that transparent or if he'd sent signals so strong that Nayo knew exactly what he wanted. He hadn't said that he wanted to sleep with her but make love to her. And for him there was a distinct difference.

Sleeping together wasn't anything more than sexual desire and gratification.

Making love translated into an emotional involvement, something that was so new to him that he was frightened. He'd thought himself in love only once in his life and it had ended badly—at least for him.

It'd taken years after losing his twin to learn to trust, to love, and his fear of loving and losing was never more apparent than when he admitted to a woman that he was falling in love with her. Even if he lived to be a hundred, Ivan would never forget the look on her face. She'd stared at him as if she'd never seen him before. After what seemed like an eon, though it was only seconds, she threw back her head and laughed in his face, telling him he was delusional. Just because she'd allowed him to sleep with her, she said, there was no need to get maudlin. Years later he'd run into her again, and she'd apologized. She'd admitted that her stepfather had sexually abused her as a child, and the trauma had left her emotionally dead. She didn't hate men, but she couldn't trust them.

For Ivan the apology had come too late. Her rejection had forced him to put up a shield to keep women at a distance. He enjoyed their company, but wouldn't permit himself to get in too deep.

Nayo took a step, pressing her chest to Ivan's. "I know, because I've been fantasizing about sleeping with you."

A wry smile twisted his mouth. She'd said *sleep,* not *make love.* "Let me know when you want to *sleep* together and I'll make it happen."

Nayo recoiled as if he'd slapped her. "Did I say something wrong, Ivan?"

"No, you didn't. You said exactly what you wanted to say."

Her temper flared. "Why the attitude, Ivan?"

"I don't have an attitude, Nayo."

"Yes, you—" A hand on her upper arm stopped her from saying whatever it was she wanted to say to Ivan. Turning, she found Geoff smiling at her. Nayo didn't have time to react when he pried her drink from her hand.

"Ivan, will you please hold Nayo's drink. This is our favorite song."

She didn't have a chance to respond before Geoff led her to a raised platform that doubled as a dance floor. "What are you doing?" she hissed as he pulled her close. She tried putting some space between their bodies, but Geoff tightened his grip around her waist.

"I'm dancing with my best friend to our favorite song," he murmured into her hair.

It took a few seconds for Nayo to recognize the Deborah Cox hit "Did You Ever Love Me?"

"It's *your* favorite song, Geoff."

Easing back, Geoff stared down at Nayo's upturned face. "You look incredibly beautiful tonight," he said for her ears only.

Nayo didn't know why, but she felt like crying. She loved Geoff but not the way a woman loved a man. She loved his giving spirit, generosity and his willingness to support her in every endeavor.

He'd put her up while she'd gone apartment hunting, refusing to take any money from her. He'd told her if she ever needed money, he would give her whatever she needed. Thankfully she hadn't had to go to him for anything. Four years of traveling across the country had taught her how to budget her funds.

"Shame on you, Geoffrey Magnus. You're here flirting with me when you should be dancing with Michiko."

His gray eyes darkened like angry storm clouds. "You know Michiko isn't who she appears to be."

"I didn't know that until Ivan pointed it out to me."

Geoff spun Nayo around and around in an intricate quick step. "Didn't I see Ivan at your showing?"

"Yes, you did."

"Do the two of you have something going?"

"We're friends, Geoff."

"The way he looks at you says he wants to be more than a friend."

"Like you?" she countered.

A beat passed. "Yes, Nayo, like me. I've never lied to you about my feelings. I'd marry you tomorrow if you'd say yes."

"I'm not going to marry you or any other man for a long time."

"Why?"

"Because I'm not where I want to be in my career."

"If you marry me, you wouldn't have to worry about your career, Nayo."

"If I marry you, I wouldn't have a career."

His brow furrowed. "Why would you say something like that?"

"Instead of being Nayo, I'd become Mrs. Geoffrey Magnus. No critic would ever take my work seriously because of the clout your family's name wields in the art world."

"That would never happen," he argued quietly.

"You're so isolated in your privileged world that you can't see beyond the zeros on your bank statement."

A flush began at Geoff's neck, creeping up his face to his hairline. "That's cruel, Nayo."

"It's true, Geoff. Do you think I could've pulled all the people who came to the showing if it hadn't been held at your gallery? No," she said, answering her own question. "Whenever Magnus Galleries opens their doors to showcase a new artist, everybody who's somebody in the art world shows up. Are they curious? Maybe. But most of them come because they want to see and be seen. I don't need some bloated, pontificating critic to tell me I'm good. The patrons who write checks are enough validation for me."

The song ended and Nayo and Geoff stood motionless, staring at each other. "I'd better take you back to your boyfriend so he can stop shooting daggers at me."

Shifting, Nayo turned to find Ivan standing with his arms crossed over his chest. His body language spoke volumes. He was not happy. "Ivan is a pussycat."

"Which one? Tiger, lion or leopard?"

"None," she said as Geoff led her back to Ivan. "One of these days I'm going to invite you over for dinner. I can tell by your face that you haven't been eating." It was thinner than she'd seen it in years.

Geoff stopped in midstride. His smile was dazzling. "You are going to let me come to your apartment?"

"Yes. I've finally finished decorating it." She'd decided to invite Geoff because Ivan had earned the distinction of being the first non-family male to enter her sanctuary.

"Can I tell you what I want you to prepare?"

Nayo placed her fingertips over his mouth. "Don't tell me now."

Geoff caught her wrist, pulling her hand away. Lowering his head, he kissed her moist lips. "Thanks."

"You're welcome." He escorted Nayo over to Ivan. "Thanks for letting me borrow your girlfriend."

Nothing on Ivan moved, not even his eyes, as he continued to glare at the tall, thin man who looked as if he would fall over in a strong wind. First the guy had had the nerve to interrupt his conversation with Nayo. Then he'd professed that their favorite song was one of unrequited love. And lastly he'd had the audacity to kiss Nayo, knowing he watched.

"Where's my drink, Ivan?"

He glared at Nayo. "I drank it."

"Where's yours?"

"I drank it."

Her round eyes grew wider. "You had two drinks in what…three or four minutes?"

"I had to do something to keep my hands occupied. Otherwise I would've pimp-slapped your skinny-ass friend."

Nayo blinked, not wanting to believe what she'd just heard. "You're kidding, aren't you?"

"Do I look like I'm kidding, Nayo?"

She rested a hand on his arm. "Come on, Ivan. There's no need for you to be jealous of Geoff and me. We've been friends for more than ten years."

"He wants more than friendship."

"I know that," she admitted.

"You know that, yet you lead the poor boy on?"

"I'm not leading him on, Ivan. We always hug and kiss."

"Would you like it if I took you out, then did a slow grind and gave a hug and kiss to a woman in front of you?"

"We weren't slow-grinding—"

"Enough, Nayo. Please."

Suddenly it dawned on Nayo. "You're jealous," she whispered.

Ivan flashed a supercilious smile. "Give that pretty lady a cigar, because she just hit the bull's-eye." He leaned in closer. "I am very, very jealous, Nayo."

"I know how that feels."

Reaching for her, Ivan pulled Nayo into the circle of his embrace. "The song that's playing is a favorite of mine. Will you dance with me?"

Nayo cocked her head, listening to the song coming through speakers set up around the loft. It was Brownstone singing "I Can't Tell You Why."

"Of course."

She followed Ivan to the dance floor and curved her arms under his shoulders. The difference of being held by him and Geoff was like night and day. She gloried in the solid muscle melding with her curves. He wanted to make love to her and she wanted to make love to him.

Ivan's hands moved down Nayo's back to her hips, pulling her even closer. He knew he was playing with fire, but he didn't care. The heat in his groin grew hotter and hotter until it became an inferno. He was on fire.

Nayo felt the pulsing hardness against her thigh and she missed a step. She would've fallen if Ivan hadn't held her up. "Ivan!"

"I know," he whispered in her ear. "It will go down."

"When?"

He chuckled. "When I get you home. I'm going to turn you around and I want you to walk in front of me until we're downstairs."

She pressed her mouth to his ear. "I should feel you up right here."

"You better not, because then I won't be the only one embarrassed tonight."

"What would you do?"

Ivan whispered in Nayo's ear what he would do to

her, eliciting the response he wanted when she gasped, "Let's go home, baby."

They managed to make it to the coat check, where an attendant gave Nayo her coat without anyone noticing Ivan's state of arousal. They were steps from the door when Geoff appeared in front of them like an apparition.

"Don't tell me you're leaving?"

Ivan shot Geoff a warning look. "Walk away, Magnus."

Geoff took a step backward. "Later, Nayo."

She nodded, rushing out of the loft in order to defuse what could've become a violent altercation. Nayo punched the button for the elevator harder than necessary.

"I don't appreciate you threatening my friend, Ivan."

"I didn't threaten him, doll face. I just told him to get out of my face."

"You were rude."

"What did you want me to say? Please go away and leave us alone because right now I have a hard-on I don't want you to see?"

Reaching around her body, Nayo grabbed his crotch. "Good grief! It hasn't gone down."

Ivan laughed, the sound coming from deep within his broad chest. "I told you it's not going down until I get you home."

The elevator arrived, and Nayo shifted to let two

costumed men exit the car. She recognized one under his Joker makeup as someone who'd been in her graduating class at the School of Visual Arts. She averted her head so he wouldn't recognize her. Fortunately they made it down to the street level without encountering anyone else.

Ivan searched in his jacket pocket for his cell phone. He punched in speed dial. "Robert, please pick us up in front of the building. Yes, we're downstairs."

Within minutes the sleek black Town Car maneuvered up to the curb. Ivan had opened the rear door before the chauffeur exited the car. Nayo got in, then he slipped in beside her. Sliding back the partition, he instructed Robert to stop at Nayo's apartment building before stopping at Melba's, a popular Harlem restaurant. He made another call, this one to Melba's. He ordered stuffed catfish, scampi with rice and collard greens, smothered pork chops, macaroni and cheese, crab cakes, string beans, corn bread and two orders of their famous chicken and waffles.

"Who in heaven's name is going to eat all that food, Ivan?" Nayo admonished him when he ended the call.

Dropping his arm over her shoulders, he pulled her close. "We are. I ordered enough for tonight's dinner and leftovers for tomorrow. We're going to stop at your place to pick up a change of clothes for you. While we're there, Robert will pick up our food. I also suggest you bring your photo equipment if you want to shoot me. If you don't have anything planned for Sunday, I'd like you to come with me to a friend's house. It's going to be very casual."

Nayo gave him a baleful look. "It looks as if you've made your own plans."

"Didn't I agree to go to the party tonight?"

"But we didn't stay."

"So, we'll have our own pre-Halloween party back at my place. And don't forget you agreed to spend Saturday with me."

"I guess I did."

"You guess right, doll face."

"Why do you call me that?"

"What?"

"Doll face."

Ivan kissed her forehead. "You have a face that reminds me of a prototype for a beautiful black doll."

Nayo wanted to tell Ivan that whenever he looked at her she felt utterly feminine and sexy. Heat warmed her cheeks as she gave him a demure smile. "Thank you."

"Don't thank me, baby. You should thank your mother and father for creating not only a brilliant daughter, but also an exquisite one."

"Stop it, Ivan, before you give me a swollen head."

"Wrong, baby. I'm the one with the swollen head."

Burying her face between his neck and shoulder, Nayo smothered the laughter bubbling up from her throat. Ivan's broad shoulders shook when his laughter joined hers. They dissolved in a paroxysm of laughter that bordered on hysterics.

She sank into her soon-to-be lover's comforting embrace, trying to remember when she'd felt so safe—safe and at peace.

Nayo believed herself one with nature when viewing the sun setting over the Grand Canyon, the grandeur of South Dakota's Black Hills, Monument Valley in Arizona—the crown jewel in the Navajo Tribal Park—and the razor-sharp summits, blue glaciers and primeval forests of Cascades National Park in the northwest corner of Washington State.

It was the same feeling she had when she was with Ivan. He'd become the yang to her yin, the black to her white and the male to her female. He complemented her in every way. All that was missing was how they would relate to each other *in* bed.

Chapter 8

Nayo emerged from the bathroom, her freshly washed face glowing. It'd taken her longer than she'd anticipated to pack an overnight bag with enough clothes to last at least two days and to gather her photographic equipment to shoot Ivan.

His driver had returned from picking up the takeout and was waiting in the car when she and Ivan came down the stairs carrying several bags. They loaded everything into the trunk of the car and less than five minutes later had to unload it again.

The delicious smells wafting from the containers reminded Nayo that she hadn't eaten anything for hours. Dyana Ryker always provided lunch for her employees, and it was usually what Nayo thought of as rabbit cuisine: lettuce and sprouts. She enjoyed eating salads but not every day. Most times she added chickpeas, slices of avocado, zucchini, tomato and occasionally crumbled feta or blue cheese to her salad greens. Not only was the dish colorful, but also healthier. It'd taken her a while to realize that some wealthy people were thin because they were genetically predisposed, but many because they simply didn't eat. There was no doubt Geoff and Dyana prescribed to the theory that one can't be too wealthy or too thin. Although she didn't and had never had a weight problem, doll face, as Ivan referred to her, liked to eat.

Wearing sock-slippers, Nayo walked out of the bedroom where she'd slept the first time she'd come to Ivan's house, and made her way to the kitchen. She smiled when she noticed that Ivan had also changed his clothes. He wore his favored Hawaiian shirt—this one in chocolate brown with bright green leaves—with a pair of cutoffs and sandals.

"Book 'em, Danno!"

Ivan turned to find Nayo standing at the entrance to the kitchen. He drew in a breath when he saw that she'd changed into a pair of pink, floral-patterned cotton lounging pants and a white tank top. It was the first time he'd seen her bare so much skin, and the effect was like a solid punch to the solar plexus. He pulled his gaze away so he wouldn't embarrass himself a second time because his body refused to follow the dictates of his brain.

He'd been honest when he told Nayo he wanted to make love to her, but that didn't translate into pounding on when the opportunity presented itself. Yes, she'd agreed to sleep at his house, but he hadn't assumed she would sleep in his bed. And he was glad he hadn't been that presumptuous, because when they'd come here after picking up her things, Nayo had carried her overnight bag to the same bedroom she'd slept in the night of the ice storm. It was nonverbal communication at its best: she wasn't ready to share his bed.

Ivan hadn't misconstrued her actions as a rejection. As a woman, an independent consenting adult, she did not have to sleep with him. He'd made it known what he wanted and he was willing to wait for Nayo to come to him. If it took days, weeks or even a month, he would wait.

What he hadn't known was he'd been waiting for years to meet a woman who wasn't afraid to speak her mind. A woman who didn't dumb herself down because some men were intimidated by her intelligence. A woman who was the epitome of femininity.

"What do you know about *Hawaii Five-O?* You couldn't have been more than a toddler when the show went off the air."

Nayo walked into the kitchen. "How would you know that, old man?" she teased. "You're not that much older than I am."

"The difference is I did get to watch the show before it went into syndication."

Nayo sat on a high stool, watching Ivan empty the bags of food. "It was, or should I say, it *is* my dad's favorite show of all time. He got hooked watching it when he dated my mother. My grandfather was sheriff of Beaver Run and he wouldn't let a boy go out with his daughter if he'd ever been picked up for driving drunk, smoking weed or speeding. I don't want to mention the other more serious infractions.

"That left very few choices from which my mother could choose. My dad was at that time the quintessential nerd and was what Grandpa referred to as 'squeaky clean.' When he gave him the go-ahead to court his daughter, instead of taking my mother to the movies or out to eat, he'd hang out with his future father-in-law talking about *Hawaii Five-O*. I gave him the boxed set for Christmas and it was something pitiful to watch a grown man go to pieces over some DVDs."

Ivan emptied the last of the bags. "I am *not* ashamed to admit that I, too, have the boxed set and I've watched the entire twelve seasons at least twice."

Nayo narrowed her eyes at him. "Twelve seasons and how many episodes?"

He shrugged. "A lot."

"How many is a lot, Ivan?"

"Two hundred eighty-four."

She closed one eye, mentally doing the math.

"You've watched 568 episodes of the same television show? That's sick, Ivan."

"I'll admit it's a little obsessive."

"It's more than a little, Dr. Campbell."

"I'm not your therapist," Ivan warned softly, "so you can dispense with the title."

"Why did you decide to become a therapist?"

"That's a long story, Nayo."

She moved closer. "We do have all weekend to get to know each other better."

"I'll tell you some other time. Now, what would you like to eat tonight?"

"Nothing too heavy. I'm not used to eating dinner this late."

Ivan glanced at the clock on the microwave. It was after ten. It *was* late. "What if we have the crab cakes and string beans tonight?"

Resting an elbow on the countertop, Nayo cradled her chin on the heel of her hand. "That sounds good."

Ivan pressed a kiss to her forehead. "You know, I never got to sample your gelato."

Nayo looked up at him through her lashes. "We can have it for dessert."

He wanted to tell Nayo that he wanted *her* for dessert. Not only dessert, but the appetizer and entrée. She was a smorgasbord he could devour in one sitting.

"Should I heat up the crab cakes and beans?"

"Yes." Nayo slipped off the stool. "You have any storage containers?"

"Yes. There should be some under the cabinet by the dishwasher."

Ivan and Nayo, working side by side, put away the food, then sat down to a dinner of crab cakes with a light cream sauce, savory string beans and scoops of pistachio gelato with cups of espresso.

"Where did you learn to make gelato?" Ivan asked Nayo. He'd found the Italian ice cream richer and smoother than traditional ice cream.

"I spent a summer in Europe and that's when I discovered gelato. Even though it's richer than ordinary ice cream and sherbet, it's less sweet and fattening. The first time I had gelato I was addicted. When I was in Rome I used to go to the same *gelateria* every day to order a different flavor. One day the owner's son, who I believe was hitting on me, offered to show me how to make it. And as they say, the rest is history. I can't remember the last time I bought or ate store-bought ice cream."

"I only had it once here in this country."

"Where was it?" Nayo asked.

"It was in Charleston, South Carolina. I've forgotten the name of the shop, but I know how to get there."

"Was it good?"

Ivan nodded. "It was delicious. I'd forgotten how much I enjoyed it until now."

"Do you have family in South Carolina?"

Ivan traced the design on the handle of his spoon with his forefinger. "My folks were originally from North Charleston. But now most of my relatives live all over the South. Some are in Atlanta, Orlando, D.C. and a few have settled in L.A."

"Where did you grow up?"

"Right here in Harlem."

Nayo gave him an incredulous stare. "You never wanted to live anyplace else?"

"Like where, Nayo?"

"Chelsea, the Village or even Battery Park?"

"No. There's a lot of history in Harlem, good history. I grew up in public housing and it was like living in a small town. Everybody knew everybody. So when someone got hooked on drugs, there was no hiding it. Or if some girl got pregnant, unless she stayed in her apartment, everyone knew it. And if she was fast, then it was, whose baby was she carrying? I suppose it was like your little town of Beaver Run, but with a lot more action."

"You never wanted to live anywhere except Harlem, while I couldn't wait to leave Beaver Run. I felt if I didn't get out, my creative spirit would die. I used to watch movies set in New York or other big cities just to hear different accents. The actors had exciting careers, wore beautiful clothes and rode in sedans and not pickups. Most kids in Beaver Run know what they're going to be before they enter adolescence. The ones who don't go to college will work in the local factories. They marry a local girl or boy, have a couple of kids, go on vacation, attend their children's graduation, weddings, bounce their grandchildren on their knees, and then they die. It wasn't that I wanted better…"

"What did you want, Nayo?"

A silence ensued before she spoke again. "I wanted more."

"Have you achieved more?"

She smiled. "Most of it."

Ivan angled his head. "How did your folks come to settle in Beaver Run?"

"My parents are descendants of runaway slaves who escaped to the North through the Underground Railroad. Daddy traces his family back to Virginia, and my mother's folks came from Tennessee. Once they crossed the Ohio River, they headed as far north as they could to escape the patrollers who were paid a bounty to bring back escaped slaves. I'd heard stories that some of my relatives wanted to go to Canada, but they ran out of food, so they settled in Beaver Run, where they hid out in the cellars of abolitionists.

"Six months later Confederate forces fired on Fort Sumter and the country erupted in civil war. Once the war ended, many freed slaves migrated north, planning to settle in Canada or other northern states. Some of them drifted through Beaver Run, and when they saw people who looked like them working on farms or in factories, they stayed and put down roots."

"Do most Beaver Run African-Americans marry each other?"

"A few do. The younger ones usually leave to go to college, and if they decide to return, it is with a husband or wife."

"Is it the bucolic little town you see on postcards?"

Nayo smiled. "Yes. It has an elementary school, but the junior- and senior-high students occupy the same building. Cheerleading, baseball and football rank up there in importance with history, calculus and chemistry. Halloween is a favorite time for kids—they really let loose. Sweet-sixteen parties are the rage for girls, and getting a driver's license is a priority for the boys, even though most of them learn how to drive as soon as their legs are long enough to reach the pedals on a tractor. Thanks to my parents' restaurant, there are no fast-food joints."

"Is there a Wal-Mart?" Ivan teased.

"Now you know there has to be a Wal-Mart. A new strip mall went up about five miles out of town, and some of the stores are giving Wal-Mart some serious competition."

"Are you saying if I go with you to visit your folks, I won't be able to get a Big Mac?"

"You can get one, but you'll have to drive a few miles."

"What do you mean by a *few?*"

"At least twenty miles."

"If there's no traditional enclosed mall, what do young kids do for fun?"

"When the strip mall went up, the family who owned the movie theater moved their base of operation and expanded to three screens, instead of the single screen, so a lot more teenagers are going to movies."

"Where do they hang out after they leave the theater?"

Ivan remembered that when he and Kyle got together with Duncan, who'd take the subway from Brooklyn, they would meet in Times Square to see a film. They would then stop at a fast-food restaurant to eat; they made certain to leave the area after nightfall, because at that time Times Square was no place for anyone who wasn't a consenting adult. It wasn't as if he could call his parents to let them know the subway or bus was delayed and he'd be home later than expected, unlike nowadays when children were given cell phones as soon as they learned to recognize numbers.

"They routinely come to the Running Beaver."

He stared, complete surprise freezing his features. "Your parents' restaurant?"

Nayo smiled at Ivan's shocked expression. She'd discovered his face was very expressive. It could be sensually brooding one minute, then flashing with a smile the next. It was like watching a sunrise.

"Unfortunately the teenagers are of the belief that having fun means either getting high or drunk. So many kids were coming to school under the influence that the town officials called an emergency town meeting to deal with the crisis. They petitioned the state for money to hire a drug-and-alcohol counselor for the high school, and parents voted to have a drug-education program become part of the school curriculum.

"A couple of years back, my brother was elected sheriff, and the town trustees worked out a deal with my father to expand the Running Beaver. He put in a soundproof room for those between the ages of thirteen to eighteen. It's equipped with flat-screen TVs showing PG-13-rated videos and movies. Dad also put in several pinball machines, and during certain hours rap and hip-hop shatter the eardrums. There's a kids' menu where the prices are considerably lower than the regular menu."

Ivan found himself enthralled by the soft sound of Nayo's voice talking about where she'd grown up. "When a guy comes in with his wife and three children and orders dinner from the regular menu, would he have to pay full price for his kids?"

"No. The children's menu applies to all children up to eighteen. The little kids can't eat or play in what they call the 'party room' until they're thirteen. And there's no need to card anyone because one thing you can't hide in Beaver Run is your age."

Ivan angled his head. "How did you know I was going to ask you that?"

"Because you're not as *miss-steery-ous* as you think you are."

Pushing back his chair, he stood up. "Go to bed, baby."

"Why?"

He began stacking dishes. "Because it's after twelve and I don't want my doll face to complain that I kept her from her beauty sleep."

Nayo rose to her feet, reaching for the espresso cups. "Let me help you clear the table."

His hands stilled and he gave her a chilling look. "I've got this, Nayo."

She detected an edge in Ivan's voice similar to the one he'd used when he'd ordered Geoff to walk away. It wasn't a warning but a threat. Nayo opened her mouth to come back at him, and then caught herself. If she said what was poised on the tip of her tongue, she knew whatever she and Ivan had shared up to that point would come to a complete and abrupt end. Bowing her head in supplication, she backed out of the kitchen to Ivan's rich, booming laughter.

Ivan was still chuckling when he rinsed and stacked dishes in the dishwasher. He finished cleaning the kitchen, but instead of going to bed, he went downstairs to his home office. To say that the night had been filled with surprises was an understatement.

He'd shocked himself when he'd gotten an erection just by dancing with Nayo. That had never happened with other women. And he'd also shocked himself with his exhibition of jealousy when he saw Nayo with Geoff Magnus. Their dancing together, hugging, laughing and kissing had tested the limits of what he'd come to recognize as a very tenuous rein on his self-control. He'd always prided himself on having command of his emotions. Most times no one could tell what he was thinking or feeling.

He'd gone at Kyle and Duncan like a charging bull when they'd mentioned not wanting to disturb him because they believed he was with a woman. Ivan lost count of the number of times the three of them went out together with whatever women they were dating at the time and wound up sleeping in his or Kyle's Harlem brownstone or at Duncan's Chelsea condo. It'd become one big slumber party with each couple sleeping in a separate bedroom.

Fortunately most of the women they dated got along with one another. The instances of *Who does she think she is* and *I can't stand that heifer* were kept to a minimum. A smile crinkled the skin around his eyes when Ivan recalled Nayo calling Michiko a heifer. She'd been jealous of Michiko and he'd been jealous of Geoffrey. However, there was one difference: he would never get involved with or sleep with the stunning-looking transvestite; but there was always the possibility that Nayo's friendship with Geoff could change from platonic to intimate.

Turning on his computer and waiting for it to boot up, Ivan recalled the day Duncan had come to him because he hadn't wanted to lose Tamara Walcott; he'd wanted to spend the rest of his life with her. He and Duncan weren't Ivan and DG but rather Dr. Campbell and patient. The impromptu counseling session concluded with Duncan going after the woman he loved, and now they were planning a June wedding.

A wry smile twisted his mouth. How had it happened? Both his friends were engaged to marry, and he—who'd dated more women than either Kyle or DG—had left a trail of them in his past.

There was a time when the three of them got together during the week and always on Sundays during football and basketball season. They were friendly rivals when it came to baseball. He and Kyle liked the Yankees, while DG was a rabid Mets fan. The rivalry intensified during the 2000 Subway Series between the two New York teams. It ended with a Yankees victory, and he and Kyle tiptoed around Duncan for weeks. The standoff ended when Duncan gave him the Waterford commemorative home plate for Christmas.

Ivan was realistic enough to know that once his friends married, their friendship would undergo a significant change. They wouldn't stop being friends, brothers. What bothered him was how long they'd have men's night out before that, too, became part of their past? DG and Kyle had talked about fathering children…

He redirected his focus to the computer and accessed his e-mail. There were eight new messages. He read them, answering half and saving four. Ivan knew exactly what he was doing when he shut down the computer. He was using avoidance. Nayo had gone to bed and he didn't want to think of her not being in his bed. Turning off the light, he headed upstairs.

"Man up, Campbell," Ivan said, sotto voce. He had to face whatever awaited him when he walked into his bedroom. A week ago he didn't know Nayo Goddard existed and it wouldn't have mattered where she slept.

His step was resolute when he approached his bedroom. Unconsciously he furrowed his brow. The door to the room was closed. Whenever he returned home to find the doors closed, he knew the cleaning staff had been there.

Placing his hand on the door handle, he opened the door, encountering darkness. He'd left the bedside-table lamp on. The sound of his quickening heart rate echoed in his ears when he detected the subtle fragrance of Nayo's perfume. She'd come to him of her own free will.

Ivan undressed, leaving his clothes on the floor near the door. Walking on bare feet, he slowly approached the bed, bumping into and hitting his right knee on the corner of the bedside table. Smothering a groan and savage expletive, he lay sprawled on the bed, holding his knee.

"What's the matter, Ivan? And why are you cursing?"

It was apparent he'd woken Nayo. "I hit my knee," he said through clenched teeth. He felt the brush of her silken skin against his arm as she moved closer.

"I'll turn on the light and take a look at it."

"Don't! I'll be all right in a few minutes."

Nayo rose on her knees, pressing her chest to his back. "Do you want me to kiss it and make it all better?"

The pain in Ivan's knee was forgotten as the sensations in another part of his body reminded him why he'd been born male. This time when he groaned it was because of the pleasurable sensations in his groin.

"Yes, baby. You can kiss it."

Wrapping her arms around Ivan's neck, Nayo trailed tiny kisses over the breadth of his shoulders, alternating the soft kisses with a gentle licking. "You smell good *and* you taste good."

Not being able to see heightened all of Ivan's senses, and he chided himself for selecting a window treatment that shut out all light. Reaching up, he caught her hands as her mouth mapped a trail down his spine.

"Easy, sweetheart."

His breathing deepened as he felt a rush of blood harden his penis, and for the second time that night he feared losing complete control. He wanted to take Nayo fast, hard and without prolonged foreplay.

Ivan inhaled sharply when Nayo's fingertips grazed

his groin in her attempt to find his knee. Like a sinewy reptile she curled around his body to lie between his outstretched legs.

"Which knee, darling?" Her voice floated in the dimness like a disembodied spirit.

"The right one."

Lowering her head, Nayo pressed a kiss to Ivan's knee. "You must have hit it pretty hard, because now there's a lump."

"Do you think I'll need round-the-clock nursing?"

Her head came up. "Do you want me to put a bandage on it?"

"Only if you promise to draw a pretty picture on the bandage."

"I have Band-Aids with cartoon characters on them."

Ivan chuckled softly. "I suppose you're still a kid at heart."

"It has nothing to do with being a kid," she argued quietly. "I happen to like pretty pictures."

Sliding up the length of his body, Nayo still lay between Ivan's outstretched legs. She could feel her blood warming from the heat of his body. He hadn't touched her intimately, yet she could feel the controlled, unleashed desire of Ivan's erection against her belly. The tremors came as softly as the silent paws of her neighbor's cat, tiny shivers that raised goose bumps on her flesh.

Ivan's arms tightened around Nayo's body when he

felt her trembling. She'd buried her face between his neck and shoulder, her curly hair tickling his nose. "What's the matter, baby?"

Nayo squeezed her eyes shut. "Nothing."

"If it's nothing, then why are you trembling?"

There was only the sound of their breathing, Nayo taking two breaths to his one as Ivan tried to analyze the slip of a woman in his bed. He didn't know it was possible, yet he felt her vulnerability.

Had he moved too quickly?

Had he pressured Nayo to sleep with him when she actually wasn't ready?

There were women who'd shared his bed within days of meeting and there were those he saw for weeks and some months that he never slept with. He'd met Nayo Goddard for the first time exactly one week ago, and he'd known then there was something special about her, other than her incredible talent.

Had he gone out with prettier women?

Yes.

More intelligent?

He doubted it.

More artistic?

Definitely not.

But none had challenged him the way Nayo did. It was as if she didn't care if he agreed or disagreed with her. She'd met him on equal footing.

The staff at the D.C. research center had called him

dictatorial. He'd hired his staff from a pool of social workers, psychologists and urban economists. They weren't just good in their field, they were the best.

Ivan had directed the program until 2002 when the center lost its contract because funds were redirected to the Defense Department to treat soldiers who'd come back from Iraq and Afghanistan exhibiting myriad mental-health problems.

"Are you a virgin, Nayo?"

"No," came her muffled reply.

"If you're not, then are you afraid of me?"

"No."

Nayo managed to free herself from his arms and lie next to him. She'd made a mistake to agree to sleep at his house. Everything she'd shared with the man in whose bed she lay had merged into one like a tightly wound spring ready to snap at any moment. She'd never permitted herself to get caught up in emotions so foreign they frightened her. She knew Ivan wanted answers, answers she wasn't certain were real or imagined.

"I am not a virgin, nor am I afraid of you, Ivan. The one I'm afraid of is myself. I meet you for the first time last Friday, and this Friday I'm in bed with you. I've never done anything like this before."

"Do you think that makes you a bad person?"

"It has nothing to do with feeling good or bad," she countered. "I've created a persona for myself that I'm just like all the other sophisticated artists who come and go, taking lovers whenever and wherever they choose while answering to no man or woman. I've lived the lie for so long that I was beginning to believe it myself. You're the first male other than my father, brother and nephew who has been in my apartment."

Ivan hadn't realized he'd been holding his breath until he felt the band of constriction across his chest. "Where do you go if you sleep with other men?"

"There have only been two others and I slept with them a long time ago. The first one was a boy I—"

"You don't have to tell me," Ivan said, interrupting her.

"But I need to tell you, Ivan."

"Okay, darling. I won't interrupt you again."

"The first boy I slept with was one I met in high school. He asked me to marry him and I accepted. He was against me leaving Beaver Run to go to college in New York City, but there wasn't anything he could do about it. I never dated or looked at another man all the while I was engaged to Jerrell. The proverbial crap hit the fan after I graduated and returned to Beaver Run to tell him that I was seriously thinking about becoming a professional photographer. What I didn't know was that he was counting on my taking over my parents' business."

"Why would he think that when you'd gone to college to become a photographer?"

Nayo smiled in the darkness. "I'm certain you're familiar the term *denial*."

Ivan laughed. "Very familiar. And as we say downstate, *da Nile* is not a river in Brooklyn." He sobered. "Why was the restaurant so important to him?"

"Jerrell's father had lost a lot of money because of bad investments and he was forced to declare bankruptcy. My fiancé felt if he married me and I took ownership of the Running Beaver, then he and his father could use it as collateral to borrow enough money to start over."

"Were they in business for themselves?"

Nayo nodded until she realized Ivan couldn't see her. "Yes. They are cabinetmakers. The armoire in my apartment is one of their designs."

"Even if you hadn't found out that he wanted to use you, do you actually believe you would've had a normal marriage with his living upstate and you down here?"

"I didn't think about that at the time because I was so in love with him. After Jerrell, I got involved with another man. What I discovered two months into the relationship was that he was married. He lived in New Jersey and worked in New York."

"How did you find out he was married?"

"One day I was sitting in his car and I saw a man's wedding band on the floor. Apparently it'd fallen out of his jacket pocket, and when I confronted him, he didn't deny it. Then he started to give me a litany of reasons why he wasn't sleeping with his wife. I stopped him after the second inane reason, told him to stop the car and I got out. I don't do well with men I sleep with, Ivan."

Shifting on his side, he pulled her to his chest. "Sleep with or make love with?"

"Make love with," she corrected.

"You know that I want to make love with you."

"And I want you, too, and I thought I was ready. When you told me to go to bed, I was heading for the guest room, then I changed my mind. I woke up to find you in bed with me. I know if I continue to see you, it's going to happen. All I ask is that you please be patient with me."

Burying his face in her hair, Ivan breathed a kiss there. "Take all the time you need. I'm not going anywhere."

Something in her plea touched a part of him he hadn't known existed, and Ivan Campbell didn't need to talk to a therapist to know that he was falling in love with Nayo Goddard.

Chapter 9

"Are you certain you don't want me to shave?"

"Stop talking, Ivan. The camera loves you just the way you are." Nayo snapped four frames in rapid succession, each one capturing the image of the man sitting on the leather chair in a white shirt unbuttoned at the throat. "Let's see a smile, handsome. That's it. Show me your pretty teeth."

Ivan stared directly at the camera. "I feel used. Exposed."

Nayo continued snapping pictures. "Now you know how women feel when they have to pose for those nasty-ass centerfolds you men love to gawk at."

"I don't buy those magazines."

Removing the camera from the tripod, she moved around to get a better angle of Ivan's lean face. "Look this way, darling."

"If you keep calling me 'darling,' I'm going to think you really like me."

"I *do* like you, darling."

"You like me, yet I'm reduced to nothing more than a piece of meat."

"Well, you're a very nice-looking piece of meat."

"Flattery will get you nowhere, doll face."

"Put your right hand over your heart, Ivan. Spread out your fingers. That's it. You're a real natural."

"Next you'll have me cradling my face like some—"

"Don't say it, Ivan. I need a few more shots and then I want you to change into the sweater." She took the shots. "That's it."

Ivan slumped against the back of the chair. "I'm blind from the flash and my mouth hurts from grinning."

Nayo removed the memory card and inserted another. "You were smiling, not grinning. The trick to offsetting the glare from the flash is to blink before each shot. Lower your eyelids before you look at the camera." Like this. She demonstrated what she wanted from him.

"Like this, baby." Ivan's eyelids fluttered wildly.

She laughed at his silly antics. "I think I'm going to

change your picture caption from 'Stunning!' to 'Stunner!'"

Ivan's hands stilled on the buttons on his shirt. "My photograph is going to be in a book?"

"Yes." Nayo peered into a case with an assortment of lenses, selected one with long-range capability. "I plan to do three books. One will be titled *Bridges*. It will be made up of the photos I don't sell, and the second one will be titled *Faces*. Your head shot and whatever pose I select will be in that one. *Places* will round out the trifecta.

"When I went on my photo expedition, my initial focus was bridges. A month into the project I decided to include landscapes and people, because I didn't want a repeat of staying in budget motels, eating in out-of-the-way places and lugging my equipment everywhere I went. Whenever I left my motel room, I took my cameras with me. If someone took my money or credit cards, I could always replace them, but not my memory cards."

Ivan unbuttoned his shirt and slipped out of it. He looked at Nayo looking at him when he reached for a wrinkled, navy-blue cotton sweater with a rolled neckline. She'd insisted the well-worn sweater and ripped jeans were perfect for the full-body shot.

Nayo explained she hadn't wanted him to shave because the two photos would be juxtaposed, one of him in a crisp white shirt and faded jeans, and the other, with the sweater, a full-body shot of him in his bare feet.

He hadn't wanted to sit for the photo session. He'd

only agreed because he wanted to prolong the time with Nayo. It was apparent his plan had backfired because he'd found himself the victim of his own erotic fantasies.

Sharing a bed with Nayo and not making love to her tested the limits of his willpower. He'd wanted her so badly that it took a long time for his erection to go down. Listening to her tell of her life in Beaver Run validated why he'd found himself drawn to her.

Under the facade of big-city sophistication was a country girl who had grown up without the angst that not speaking to strangers or knowing one's neighbor caused. People were people regardless of the region in which they resided and society's ills didn't discriminate as to region, gender or social status. Beaver Run wasn't so isolated that it had been spared the pain associated with substance abuse or teenage pregnancies, but the number of incidents were minute when compared to the number in bigger cities. The town officials hadn't denied there was a problem. They'd addressed it by including drug education in the curriculum, and instead of building a playground for their youth to work off excess energy, they'd provided them with a space where they could hang out with adult supervision.

Ivan had felt Nayo's vulnerability and respected her willingness to open up to him. She'd asked him to be patient with her and he would be. Gaining her trust was the key if they were to have a relationship.

Nayo forced herself not to stare at Ivan's rock-hard

abs as he pulled the tattered sweater over his head. She bit down on her lip to stop its trembling. What she couldn't stop was the clenching and unclenching of her stomach muscles or the soft pulsing between her legs.

She'd gotten out of bed before Ivan. The window shades hadn't permitted her to see the magnificence of his nude body. She knew she'd had to leave his bed before she changed her mind and begged him to make love to her.

Nayo had been honest when she admitted she was uncomfortable sharing his bed after knowing him a week. She wasn't a prude, yet something wouldn't permit her to open her legs to a stranger.

She attributed her dating Jerrell for a year before she gave him her virginity to immaturity. The thing that had frightened her most was that he would brag to his friends that he'd "popped her cherry." Nayo lost count of the number of girls in her high school who were outted when boys they'd slept with bragged about their conquests.

Nayo had slept with the married man when she was on the rebound from her breakup with Jerrell. If not him, she had no doubt she would've slept with another man. It was as if she needed to exorcise Jerrell from her mind and her body.

Setting her camera on the tripod, Nayo walked over to Ivan. She'd decided to photograph him against a wall in the living room. The wall doubled as the screen she would've used at a studio. His photo, like the others, would be shot in black and white. Unlike some photographers, Nayo didn't plan to retouch his face. Whatever imperfections the camera lens captured would remain.

"I need you to lean against the wall with your left shoulder tilted slightly toward me. You can slip your hands in the front pockets of your jeans, pulling them down slightly. Don't worry," she said when he gave her a pointed look, "the hem of the sweater is long enough to cover your belly. Now, cross your left foot over your right."

"I don't want to look like I'm selling something," Ivan grumbled.

She rolled her eyes. "You've the face and body of a model, darling. So stop bitchin' and moanin'."

"I'm too old to model."

"No, you're not. Male models are not just young boys. If you weren't so prudish, I'd shoot you without a top."

Ivan smarted from her comment. Waiting until she walked back to the tripod, he reached down and pulled his sweater over his head, letting it fall to the floor beside his feet. He raised his arms over his head, grasping his wrists.

It took only seconds for Nayo to react to the erotic pose. The waistband of the jeans slipped lower, displaying a flat belly. She could count every muscle in his six-pack abdomen. She took frame after frame of the defined muscles in his powerful upper arms.

Ivan changed position and she shot him with his

head angled to the right and then to the left. He was blessed with a face equally photographic on both sides. The lens captured the unabashed beauty of his toned pectorals when he crossed his arms over his chest. She continued to shoot when he bent over to pick up the sweater, the muscles in his back flexing with the smooth motion.

Photographing Ivan Campbell was akin to making love. The sensations started slowly, quickening until the building passion screamed for release. Nayo removed the camera from the tripod. Going to one knee, she shot Ivan from a lower position. There was no part of his body she hadn't captured for posterity. A soft beeping indicated she'd filled up the memory card.

Sitting on the floor, head lowered, she took deep breaths to still the beating of her runaway heart. What she'd just shared with Ivan would be imprinted on film and on her brain—forever.

Ivan pushed away from the wall and sank to the floor beside Nayo. He knew what she was feeling because he felt the same way—a sexual tension that begged to be assuaged.

Taking the camera from her limp fingers, he set it aside and gathered her to his chest. "Baby," he whispered over and over.

Nayo's head came up, and what she saw in the dark eyes gazing back at her sent another shock of awareness through her body. "Love me," she whispered seconds before her mouth met his in a burning kiss that stole the breath from her lungs.

"Are you sure?" Ivan asked, his voice lowering an octave. He had to ask her, because he didn't want a repeat of the night before. There was no way he could walk around with another erection without seeking a respite from the sexual frustration.

She nodded. "I'm very sure."

He gathered Nayo off the floor and carried her out of the living room and down the hall to his bedroom, aware that he had to go slow with her. She'd revealed that it had been a while since she'd slept with a man. Vanity surfaced, leading him to believe that Nayo had saved herself for him.

Pride filled his chest when he thought about the woman in his arms. She was perfect, exquisite, and now he understood what his friends had said they'd felt when they met their respective fiancées for the first time.

Kyle couldn't stop talking about Ava Warwick, and whenever Ivan saw them together, he knew they shared a special bond. Soul mates.

Duncan had finally come to grips with losing his first fiancée, and had accepted that his life didn't stop with the first woman with whom he planned to spend his future. Kalinda Douglas was gone and was never coming back, but it wasn't until the financial planner met Dr. Tamara Walcott that he was able to let go of the past to share his love and life with her.

Ivan had asked himself over and over if Nayo was *the one*. Was she the woman to make him let go of his past of loving and losing, and commit to her and their future together?

Pinpoints of light came through the mesh shades, dotting the walls and every solid surface. Ivan lowered Nayo to the bed, his body following hers down. "Please look at me, Nayo." Her eyes opened and she smiled. "Once we do this we'll never be the same."

Nayo's smile grew wider. She didn't want to be the same Nayo Goddard she'd been before coming face-to-face with Ivan Campbell. "I know that, darling."

Ivan winked at her. "Just checking," he said.

Slowly, methodically, he undid the buttons on her blouse, baring an expanse of flawless dark skin that glistened as if sprinkled with diamond dust. Lowering his head, he kissed her silken throat before moving lower to leave a trail of kisses along the column of her slender neck. Nayo hadn't worn a bra and her small, firm breasts were on display for his visual pleasure.

He ran his first and second finger down her breast-bone, eliciting a slight shiver, which he felt under his fingertips. He'd become a sculptor, tracing the dips and curves of her body. Ivan's mouth was as busy as his hands. Every place he touched he followed with a kiss. Lost in the rising desire he derived from touching and kissing Nayo, Ivan tried to think of everything else but the exquisite body under his. Somehow he succeeded when he was able to divest her of her clothes and he still hadn't sustained a complete erection.

His rapacious gaze moved slowly over her body. "One of these days you're going to have to show me how to use your camera so I can photograph you in the nude."

Sitting back on his knees, he pulled the sweater up and over his head and shoulders. Nayo's hands stopped his when they went to the waistband of his jeans.

"Please let me do this."

Nayo felt the heat of his gaze on her lowered head. Ivan had no idea what it meant for her to take the initiative in what would become the most intimate act between a man and woman. In the past she'd merely been a willing participant, giving her partner the lead.

Ivan claimed they'd never be the same after making love, but he was wrong. He hadn't penetrated her and yet she wasn't the same Nayo she'd been the night before. She wasn't the same woman she'd been before setting up the shoot.

Whenever she peered through a camera lens, she didn't recognize herself as the girl who'd come from Beaver Run. She was Nayo, a photographer who went by a single name like Prince or Madonna. She'd become an artist, stepping outside herself in order to step into a role where she didn't use her voice or paints and brushes. She used the gift of sight to see what others couldn't or wouldn't see. It only took a glance to mentally photograph a subject.

It'd been that way when she first saw Ivan. The first thing she recognized was the perfection of his hands. They were well-groomed, the fingers long and slender. His clothes were mere window dressing for an exquisitely proportioned body the world would come to know when she developed the prints.

Unsnapping the waistband, Nayo undid the zipper. Ivan facilitated her removing his jeans by lifting his hips. Her heart beat a wild tattoo against her ribs. The bulge in the black boxer-briefs revealed that he was fully aroused.

Ivan rose slightly. Nayo's hands were shaking. "You can't stop now, darling."

Hands moving as if in slow motion, Nayo hooked her fingers in the waistband of his briefs, pulling them down Ivan's hips. What lay before her eyes became imprinted on her brain. And in that instant she wished she'd shot him nude. His erection was as impressive as the rest of his body. Moving up that body, she lay between his legs as she had the night before. This time it was her bare breasts pressed to his naked chest.

Reaching down, Ivan cupped her hips, massaging them in an up-and-down motion. Within seconds he could detect the scent of desire rising from her. "If there's anything you don't want me to do, then I want you to tell me."

"Don't talk, Ivan. Just do it."

Reversing positions, he lay between her legs, his mouth charting a sensual path under her armpits, down her rib cage. He tasted her breasts, his teeth teasing the nipples until they hardened to ripe dark points.

Nayo's fingers tightened in the mound of pillows cradling her shoulders. What Ivan was doing to her with his mouth made her feel as if she was losing her mind. A swathe of heat swept down her body with the intensity of an inferno, and she found it impossible to stop her hips from writhing in a rhythm that needed no rehearsing or tutoring.

"Please, Ivan!"

Her last words were smothered on her lips when Ivan covered her mouth with his. He moved his tongue in and out of her mouth, simulating his making love to her. Reaching over to the drawer in the bedside table, he grasped a condom. His mouth still affixed to hers, he managed to open it. Lifting his hips slightly and using both hands, he slid the latex sheath down the length of his erect penis.

He'd told Nayo they would never be the same the moment he penetrated her, but he knew he hadn't been the same man since walking into the art gallery and meeting the brilliant photographer for the first time.

He applied pressure to her thigh and settled himself between her spread legs. Positioning the head of his penis against her opening, Ivan pushed gently into her vagina, her breathing quickening against his ear. The instant he attempted to penetrate Nayo's body he knew she was different. And the difference had nothing to do with sex.

Ivan had encountered women who'd suggested threesomes, even a few foursomes, some who favored bondage with whips and chains and other acts that would classify them as sexual deviants.

As soon as he attempted to penetrate Nayo's body, he forgot every other woman he'd ever known, dated or made love to. It was as if he'd been on a pilgrimage, searching in earnest for that one woman to complete him.

Her soft moans and gasps as he eased his erection into her tight flesh left him shaking with a pleasure he'd never known. He felt as if he'd been waiting all of his life for Nayo, that he'd had to sleep with the other women in order to recognize when he'd met the right one.

Nayo had confessed to having only two lovers. This appealed to his ego because she hadn't come to him with a number of men in her past. Burying his face in her neck, he placed a kiss under her ear.

"Easy, baby," he murmured, hoping to prevent her from having any pain as he attempted to sheathe himself fully inside her. "Am I hurting you?" he whispered. She was as tight as a virgin.

Breathing heavily through parted lips, Nayo shook her head. "No." It wasn't the pain she couldn't withstand, but the carnal pleasure that she didn't want to stop. Ivan was much larger than her two previous lovers. And yet she feared climaxing because it would end much too quickly for her.

She raised her hips to receive Ivan's kiss, while he made one strong final thrust that left him buried deeply within her flesh. They sighed in unison.

Easing back, Ivan smiled at the woman tucked under his body. They shared a knowing smile, the silent gesture conveying that they'd become one with the other. "Are you ready?" he asked in a quiet voice.

"I think I was ready the night you walked into the gallery."

Ivan's smile grew wider. "I suppose I'm a little slower, because I consciously repressed my feelings. I didn't realize how much I actually wanted you until I saw you with your bohemian boyfriend."

It took Nayo several seconds to realize Ivan was referring to Geoff. Although Geoff had long hair and lived in the Village, he was anything but bohemian. He went through phases where he'd grow his hair long, then when his patrician grandmother complained about his appearance, he cut it. As heir to a collection of priceless art, Geoff knew when to rebel and when to conform.

Pressing her mouth to Ivan's strong neck, Nayo closed her eyes. "There's no need for you to be jealous of Geoff."

Ivan chided himself for bringing the man up. He'd never been one to have a third person in his bed, whether tangible or intangible. He moved his hips, Nayo following his lead as if they'd done their dance of desire countless times.

Nayo melted into the firmness of the mattress as Ivan's lips caressed hers, eliciting delicious sensations that started at her toes and swept up to her chest like a sirocco sweeping across a dry, hot desert.

Anchoring her arms under his shoulders, she held on to Ivan as he set a slow, sensual rhythm that quickened, slowed and quickened again. His lips traced a path from her mouth to her throat and along her shoulders. She was on fire!

Nayo moaned softly, then bit her lip to stop its trembling as shivers of delight gripped her tightly, held for several seconds before releasing her. She writhed as wave upon wave of erotic pleasure pulsed through her body, leaving her gasping in sweet agony. She'd fantasized about Ivan making love to her, but her fantasies paled in comparison to the reality.

Ivan couldn't believe the pleasure he derived from the tight warmth of Nayo's body, the way her flesh opened and closed around him, milking him until he was unable to hold back his climax. Cupping her hips in his palms, he lifted her higher to allow for deeper penetration.

Then without warning, Nayo screamed his name, the sound lingering in the silence of the bedroom and making the hair on the back of his neck stand up. Their bodies were so attuned to each other that when she cried out for release, his deep moans overlapped hers.

They lay together, breathing in deep lungfuls of

air. If he hadn't recently had a complete physical, Ivan would've thought that he was having a heart attack. Waiting until his breath resumed a normal rhythm, he pressed his mouth to the column of Nayo's moist neck.

Although he'd known there was something special about the photographer the moment he met her, he'd never imagined he'd fall in love with her. Even as a therapist, he didn't want to analyze why Nayo Goddard and not some other woman.

Now he knew what Duncan and Kyle were bragging about when they claimed they were able to recognize that special woman who would make them commit and plan for a future that included marriage and children.

It'd taken only a week for him to recognize that Nayo was his special woman, a woman he wanted to spend the rest of his life with, a woman he wanted as his wife, life partner and the mother of their children.

"I'll be right back," he whispered, loath to withdraw from her warm body.

Ivan slipped off the bed and went into the adjoining bathroom to discard the condom. When he returned, he found Nayo on her side with her back to him, asleep. Climbing into bed, he looped an arm around her waist and they lay together like spoons.

"Thank you," she whispered.

Ivan smiled. He thought she'd fallen asleep. "You're welcome."

Those were the last two words he said as he closed his eyes, joining Nayo in the sated slumber reserved for lovers.

Chapter 10

"Now I know you really like me," Nayo said as she smoothly maneuvered Ivan's Stingray to the curb only feet from Kyle Chatham's Georgian-inspired home along the street known as Strivers' Row.

"Why's that?" Ivan asked.

"You let me drive your mistress."

"That's where you're wrong, doll face. I'd never equate an inanimate object to my mistress."

Nayo shut off the engine, handing Ivan the keys. When she'd suggested taking a taxi to Kyle's house, Ivan rebuffed her suggestion, saying he was driving. They'd walked three blocks to the garage where he kept his car, and when the attendant exited the twenty-four-hour garage driving the classic sports car, she couldn't conceal her surprise. Her brother, who collected, restored and sold classic cars, owned the same model as Ivan. Even the gleaming black paint job was the same.

"Most guys I know wouldn't let a woman touch their cars," she said. "I knew a few who wouldn't let a woman even *sit* in their precious vehicles." The word *vehicles* came out in three distinct syllables.

"Any time you want to drive it, you can."

Nayo waited as Ivan got out of the low-slung car and came around to the driver's side to assist her. Extending his hand, he pulled her gently to her feet. Then he gathered her in a close embrace and kissed her.

"Get a room, Campbell!" shouted a deep voice a short distance away.

Ivan eased back but didn't drop his arms when he saw Duncan Gilmore, who'd just gotten out of a taxi. His fiancée stood at his side, smiling. "Mind your neck, DG," he teased, smiling broadly.

Nayo knew she was staring at the man Ivan called DG, but she couldn't help it. The man was past fine. He was gorgeous! And the tall woman standing next to him was his female counterpart. Her thick, dark, chemically straightened hair was pulled off her face and secured with a narrow, black-velvet ribbon. She and the man Ivan called DG shared the same olive-tawny complexion, but whereas DG's eyes were a clear gold color hers were a deep brown.

Duncan Gilmore stepped forward, extending his hand to Nayo. "Duncan Gilmore. This lady is Tamara Walcott."

Ivan's arm tightened around Nayo's waist. She wore a bottle-green, sheepskin-lined, three-quarter swing coat. "DG, Tamara, this is Nayo Goddard."

Nayo shook hands with Duncan and Tamara. "It's nice meeting you."

Ivan lowered his head, kissing Nayo's hair. "Why don't you and Tamara go inside? I'll get DG to help me bring in the wine and dessert."

Waiting until Nayo and Tamara disappeared into the three-story, buff-brick building with white-stone trim, Ivan turned to see Duncan staring at him. He knew his friend was curious about Nayo.

"What, DG?"

"What what, Ivan?"

"I guess you want to know about her?"

Duncan, crossing his arms over the front of his bulky sweater, affected an expression of indifference. "Did I ask about her, Ivan? You know I can't keep up with the number of women you hang with."

"This one is special." The admission came out before Ivan could censor himself.

"How special, brother?"

Ivan ducked his head, smiling. "Very, very special. Now I know what you were talking about when you met Tamara. Nayo's different from the others."

Duncan lifted his silky eyebrows. "We'll see."

"Hold up, DG. What do you mean by 'We'll see'?"

"I've lost count of the number of women I've seen you with over the years. To me, Nayo is just another one to add to the names and faces I've forgotten."

Ivan's expression mirrored his annoyance and resentment. He'd always been there for Duncan, especially when he'd lost his mother and his fiancée, and he was annoyed at DG's cynical response.

"Forget it, DG." He went back to the Corvette. "Help me bring something inside."

Duncan Gilmore hesitated, then followed his friend. He knew Ivan was upset with him. But how did he expect him to react? He'd never heard "love them and leave them" Ivan Campbell talk about any woman being special.

He'd known Ivan to date a woman once or twice, then move on to the next. It was as if he feared committing to one woman. Even Kyle had engaged in relationships of long duration, had been, in fact, the only one of the three friends to propose marriage before his thirtieth birthday.

"I'm sorry, Ivan."

"What the hell are you apologizing about?"

Duncan stared at the familiar mask of indifference that turned his best friend into a stranger. "I didn't mean to minimize your feelings for Nayo."

Ivan picked up a case of wine, shoving it at Duncan. "Take that inside." The two men stared at each other with what might've become a visual beat-down. The beginnings of a smile flitted across his features. "Apology accepted."

Duncan smiled back. "She's cute. There's something about her that reminds me of Ava."

"It's probably the short hair and their coloring." Ivan lifted a large box filled with delicate Italian pastries.

"Where did you meet her and how long have you two been together?"

"I'll tell you later," Ivan said when he saw Kyle Chatham standing in the doorway.

Nayo felt as if she'd known Ava Warwick and Tamara Walcott for years when she sat in the ultramodern black-and-white kitchen with the two women, She noticed the exquisite diamond engagement rings on their left hands.

The three had settled on stools at the cooking island sipping wine and munching on assorted crostinis with tomato and basil, spicy shrimp, white bean with sage and avocado and goat cheese, while the men retreated to a room in the rear of the house to watch football.

Ava rolled her slanting dark eyes. "Eight more weeks and then it will be over," she whispered.

Tamara sucked her teeth loudly. "Don't forget there's still the Super Bowl."

Nayo studied the two women. Ava Warwick, a social worker, and E.R. doctor Tamara Walcott were engaged to marry Kyle Chatham and Duncan Gilmore the following year. She and Ava both had short hair and similar coloring, but Ava was taller, her body fuller than Nayo's. Tamara's was statuesque, her figure full and undeniably womanly.

"Don't remind me," Ava drawled. "Kyle said he was going to try to get tickets for the Super Bowl for himself, Jordan, Duncan and Ivan."

Tamara took a sip of wine, while peering over the rim of her glass at Ava. "Duncan didn't mention anything to me about going to the Super Bowl." She turned to Nayo. "Did Ivan say anything to you about the Super Bowl?"

Nayo shook her head. "Not a word." How could she tell them that she had just met Ivan and didn't know enough about him?

Tamara reached for another crostini. "How did you meet Ivan?"

"He came to a gallery where I had a showing of photographs."

Ava sat up straighter. "You're a photographer?"

Nayo smiled. "Yes."

"I'm still looking for a photographer for my wedding," Ava said. "My wedding planner has tried to get a good one, but all seemed to be booked."

"When and where are you getting married?"

"It's scheduled for Valentine's Day in San Juan, Puerto Rico. If you're coming with Ivan, it would work out perfectly."

"Don't you want to see my work, Ava?" Nayo asked.

"How was your showing?"

A beat passed as Nayo gazed at Ava. "It was very successful."

Ava waved her hand. "If it makes you feel more comfortable, I'll look at your work. Meanwhile, don't book any events for that day."

Shifting slightly on the stool, Nayo gave Tamara a questioning look. "Do you also need a photographer?"

Tamara touched the corners of her mouth with a napkin. "I'm not getting married until June, so it's not too early to talk about photographers. I'd like to see your work, then Duncan and I will make a decision."

"Where are you getting married?" Nayo asked her.

"We're getting married aboard a ship here in the city. Duncan has already reserved space on the *Celestial*."

"Are you both using the same wedding planner?"

Tamara and Ava shared a smile. "Yes," they chorused.

"Kyle mentored the husband of the owner of Signature Bridals when he was in law school," Ava said proudly.

"Do you know how difficult it is to become a Signature bride?" Nayo asked. "I've heard rumors that the mother of a prospective bride offered to pay Signature Bridals a cool million dollars to bump another bride from a particular wedding date so her daughter could have it."

"Did Tessa Whitfield-Sanborn take it?"

"The last I heard she refused to take the woman's telephone calls."

Tamara shook her head. "Now that's what you call ballsy. Didn't the woman know that some people just can't be bought, no matter the price?"

"Thank goodness for that," Ava drawled.

Tamara gave Ava a knowing look. "You're talking smack because you're going to be a Signature bride."

"So are you," Ava countered.

"Only because your man knows the husband of the owner," Nayo said.

Raising her wineglass, Ava toasted Nayo. "You're right about that. It's not *what* you know, it's *who* you know."

"Here, here," Nayo and Tamara chorused, touching glasses.

Kyle Chatham strolled into the kitchen. When Ivan had introduced Nayo to the attorney, he didn't shake her hand, but kissed her cheek while welcoming her to his home. He was the perfect prototype for tall, dark and handsome. The sprinkling of gray in his cropped hair only served to enhance his good looks.

"What's on the menu for halftime snacks?"

Ava pointed to a tray of crostini. "We're having these."

Kyle's eyes narrowed as he peered closely at the small circles of toasted baguettes. "Is that it?"

Ava gave him an incredulous look. "Yes, that's it. What were you expecting?"

"I thought you were going to make buffalo wings with an assortment of chips and dips, not these little froufrou doodads."

"Tamara said crostini is healthier than wings."

Nayo exchanged a glance with Tamara. It was as if they'd connected telepathically. As if on cue, they slipped off their stools and prepared to leave the kitchen, but Kyle's outburst impeded their smooth escape.

"Healthier!" he shouted.

"What's the holdup, Kyle?" Ivan asked, walking into the kitchen, Duncan several steps behind him.

Kyle gave his friends a wry smile. "The *ladies* have decided we need to eat healthier. Therefore our halftime cuisine is itty-bitty French bread topped with veggies."

"No wings?" Ivan and Duncan said in unison. Their crestfallen expressions were priceless.

Clapping a hand over her mouth, Nayo was able to muffle the laughter bubbling up from her throat. She couldn't believe grown men were acting like children because they were denied their favorite party food.

Duncan shook his head. "We get together once a week to watch football, and this is the first time we've been subjected to halftime lockdown."

Ivan, muscular arms crossed over a black, crew-neck, cashmere sweater, glared at Kyle. "Handle your woman, Chatham."

"It's not Ava," Kyle said.

"Then who is it?" Duncan asked. The expression on his face was disbelief.

Ivan stared at Nayo. "I know it's not *my* woman, so it has to be yours, DG."

Duncan slapped his forehead with the heel of his hand. "Baby, you didn't."

Tamara rested her hands on her hips. She wore a pair of chocolate-brown stretch pants and a man-tailored white shirt. Overhead recessed light caught the brilliance of the emerald-cut diamond on her left hand. "Yes, I did. You have to learn to eat healthier."

A rush of color flooded Duncan's face, and his eyes appeared lighter than they actually were. "I eat healthy six days a week, and we are entitled to have a halftime snack once a week. And you're lucky football has a short season. We could do this for every Yankee and Mets home game." He looked at Ivan for support. "What if we meet at your place next Sunday for our MNO?"

"What's an MNO?" Nayo asked.

"Men's night out," Kyle explained.

Nayo's eyebrows lifted. "I see." It was apparent that whenever the three men got together, they determined beforehand whether they would include their women.

Ivan met Nayo's eyes. He was in a quandary. He always enjoyed hanging out with Kyle and Duncan, but that was before he'd met Nayo. His lifelong friends were his brothers; they would always have one another's back, but things had changed. They all operated their own businesses out of the same building, yet they spent less downtime together. It was something he attributed to being an employer, rather than an employee.

Things had also changed because his two friends were engaged to be married, and their personal focus was now their future wives and eventually children. Ivan hadn't realized it until today, but he wanted what Kyle and Duncan had: a stable relationship with one woman. Duncan's comment that he hadn't been able to keep up with the number of women he'd seen Ivan with over the years had cut to the quick.

Had he dated a lot of women?

Yes.

Had he slept with a lot of women?

No.

Had he fallen in love with any of them?

No.

He *had* professed to love one woman in his past, but realized after they parted that it was mere infatuation, more lust than love. What he felt for Nayo was different. She'd changed him inside and out. She'd softened his gruff exterior, making him laugh when he hadn't wanted to laugh.

"What's up, Ivan?" Duncan asked. "Are we going to meet at your place next Sunday?"

"I'm not able to commit right now. I have to check with Nayo."

Duncan opened his mouth to challenge Ivan, but caught his fiancée's warning look. "We'll talk about it tomorrow."

Ava placed a spicy shrimp crostini on a napkin and handed it to Kyle. "Try this."

He popped the small appetizer into his mouth, chewing slowly. A smile spread across his handsome features. "Hey, that's good." He pointed to another on the platter. "What's this one?"

"Tomato and basil, darling," Ava crooned.

Ivan moved closer to the platter, peering at the crostini. "I'll take one with tomato and basil."

Ava waved her hand in a gesture of dismissal. "Why don't you guys go back and watch your game? I'll bring you a plate." Waiting until the men retreated, she flashed a grin. "It worked, Tamara."

Tamara gave Ava a soft fist bump. "What's up with Ivan?" she whispered. "I'd expected him to step up and offer his house for next week, but he didn't."

Ava gave Nayo a long, penetrating stare. "I think Miss Nayo here has something to do with that. What's up, girl?"

Nayo felt her face suffuse with heat as she sat down again. "Nothing."

Tamara sucked her teeth. "Don't be so modest, Nayo. Your man is whipped."

Nayo did not respond to Tamara's quip, because she didn't *have* a response. Ivan wasn't her man just because they'd slept together, and she didn't know him well enough to determine if he'd mellowed.

"I know how to make buffalo wings without deep-frying them," she said, instead.

"How?" Ava asked.

"You can use the same oven-bake method as you would with chicken. I usually coat them with Japanese *panko* bread crumbs after spraying them with a garlic-infused peanut oil. *Panko* crumbs are lighter than traditional bread crumbs, stay crisp longer and are healthier because they contain less salt and calories."

"Okay," Tamara drawled. "You could be onto something, Nayo. Maybe the guys can have their wings while eating healthier at the same time."

"Tamara's right," Ava said. "Nayo, why don't you convince Ivan to host next Sunday's football outing and you make your *panko* buffalo wings?"

"Where did you learn about *panko* bread crumbs?" Tamara asked Nayo.

"My parents own a restaurant."

"Where?" Ava asked.

"It's upstate."

Tamara squinted at her. "How far upstate?"

"It's about forty miles from Lake Placid."

Ava whistled softly. "Really upstate. How would you get there if you're not driving?"

"I fly into the Adirondack regional airport and someone picks me up from there."

Tamara reached for the bottle of wine and topped off everyone's drinks. "How long have you known Ivan?"

Nayo had been anticipating the question. If she were to bond with the fiancées of Ivan's two friends, then she had to be honest. "A week."

"A week," Ava repeated. "It's only been a week and he's deferring to you. Nice going, Nayo."

"What are you talking about?" Nayo knew she sounded defensive, but she hadn't wanted the two women to misconstrue her relationship with Ivan.

"You've turned your man into a teddy bear," Ava said, smiling. "I've heard Ivan is an excellent therapist, but when he's not being Dr. Campbell, the man can be quite formidable. The first time I met him I felt as if I was being interrogated. It didn't take long for me to realize he was just being protective of his friend."

"Don't you mean brother?" Tamara asked. "Ivan, Duncan and Kyle are tighter than most brothers." She set her wineglass on the countertop next to the double sink. "I better stop drinking or I'll mess up dinner."

Tamara, wiping crumbs off the granite surface with a napkin, asked, "What's for dinner?"

"I decided to go down South tonight. We'll start with a seafood gumbo, collard greens, blackened red-snapper filets and corn bread," said Ava.

Nayo slid off her stool. "Do you have filé powder?" she asked Ava.

"No, I don't. Why?"

"Gumbo is not gumbo without filé powder."

Ava grimaced. "I'd send one of the guys out to the supermarket to pick up some, but I don't want the proverbial mess to hit the fan."

"I'll ask Ivan," Nayo volunteered.

"Good luck, girl," Tamara muttered. Once Duncan zeroed in on the sports channel, nothing short of a nuclear explosion could distract him.

Nayo made her way past rooms filled with exquisite furnishings selected for comfort and entertaining. She approached the room where the three men sat on a leather grouping watching football on a large, wall-mounted television. Pockets doors were closed, and although she could see their mouths moving, she couldn't hear what they were saying. It was obvious the room had been soundproofed.

She opened the door and the surround-sound system came at her like the roar of a jet engine. The volume was turned up so high that Nayo felt as if she were in a movie theater. Somehow she managed to get Kyle's attention and he used a remote control to lower the volume.

"I'd like to see Ivan for a minute."

Ivan rose to his feet when he heard Nayo's voice. He went over to her. "What's the matter, sweetheart?"

"I'm sorry to bother you, but I need you to go to the store and buy some filé powder. I'm making gumbo."

He stared down at the woman who within the span

of a week had turned his life upside down. What he was beginning to feel for her was so intense it was palpable. Ivan didn't want to admit that he was falling in love with Nayo Goddard, but that was the only word he could come up with to identify the sensation he had whenever they occupied the same space. Reaching out, he brushed a curl off her forehead.

"Is there anything else you'll need?"

"No. That's it." Nayo gave him gentle smile. "Thank you."

Cradling her face in his palms, he lowered his head and brushed a kiss over her parted lips. "You're welcome." He watched Nayo retreat, and then turned to see Duncan and Kyle staring at him with more interest than they had in the game. "I have to go to the supermarket."

Kyle gave him a questioning look. "I thought Ava and I bought everything she needed yesterday."

"Nayo said she needs some filé powder to make gumbo."

"And you're going in the middle of the game?" Duncan asked.

"Stay out of it, Gilmore," Kyle warned softly. "Somebody told me that your woman sent you to the store to pick up a home pregnancy kit."

Ivan chuckled. "Now that's where I draw the line. I stay out of the feminine-products aisle."

"You and DG are still whipped," Kyle crowed.

"And you're not?" Duncan countered. "Face it, brothers. We are all whipped!"

Duncan and Kyle touched fists, silently acknowledging that falling in love with the right woman was worth wearing the letter *W* around their necks.

Chapter 11

Nayo hummed along with the song coming from a built-in speaker in the kitchen as she melted butter in a heavy skillet before adding flour, then liquid to make a roux. She concentrated on stirring the mixture until it was light caramel in color. It'd been a while since she'd made a roux, and she'd forgotten how long it took to make it perfectly smooth.

Tamara had washed three bunches of collard greens. She'd stacked the leaves, rolled them together lengthwise in a tight bundle and cut them crosswise into one-inch strips. "Ava, do you want to cook the greens in the pressure cooker?"

Ava glanced up. She'd just finished shucking oysters and peeling shrimps for the gumbo. "No. I prefer the longer, stove-top method. Kyle told me they plan to watch two games, so it's going to be a while before we sit down to dinner."

Nayo took the pot with the roux off the heat and set it aside. "Should I make the gumbo mild or spicy?"

"How spicy is spicy?" Tamara asked.

Nayo smiled. "I can either use this whole can of diced tomatoes and green chilies or half."

"I don't know about Ivan and Duncan, but Kyle likes heat," Ava said as she washed her hands in one of two stainless-steel sinks.

"Ivan has Tabasco sauce in his house, so I assume he uses it." Nayo knew she'd opened herself up to endless questions about her and Ivan, although she'd admitted to meeting him a week ago.

What Nayo found puzzling was that she hadn't experienced guilt after sleeping with Ivan, then realized it wasn't the length of time two people knew each other, but how they related to and respected the other.

She'd known Jerrell all her life, yet she hadn't actually *known* him. If she'd been aware that he wanted to use her for financial gain, she never would've consented to go out on the first date.

There wasn't much she could say about her duplicitous married lover. If she'd looked harder, she would've recognized the signs that indicated that a so-called single man was just the opposite: he only gives you his cell or office number, you can't reach him on weekends—because he's probably with his wife and children—and all of the liaisons are conducted at your place. Nayo had called herself the fool of fools, but it had been too late. For the second time in her life a man had used her.

However, she didn't intend to repeat the mistake with Ivan. He had two important things in his favor: he didn't need her money and he obviously wasn't married.

"Turn that up," Tamara said, snapping her fingers in time to "In da Club," the catchy, classic, hip-hop club favorite.

Ava swung a dish towel above her as she cut a step. "I lost track of how many times I danced to this record." Nayo joined her, and soon the three women were gyrating and sliding across the black-and-white vinyl tiles on the kitchen floor as if they were in a dance club.

The chiming of the telephone penetrated the driving bass beat, and Ava turned down the radio to answer the call. Reaching for a pen, she made notes on a nearby pad, then hung up. The call had lasted less than a minute.

She ran a hand over the short hair on the nape of her neck. "Ladies, if you haven't already, please don't plan anything the Saturday of the Thanksgiving weekend."

Tamara rolled her eyes. "I think I'm scheduled to work that weekend."

"Can you get off?" Ava asked.

"What's happening that weekend?"

"Signature Bridals' floral designer is renewing her vows. Simone Whitfield and her delicious-looking husband got married in Vegas in August."

"But that was only three months ago," Nayo said.

Ava smiled. "That would be all right for people who aren't in the wedding business. The Whitfields have been in the business for more than thirty years, and getting married at a Vegas chapel with a James Brown or Elvis impersonator as a witness doesn't sit very well with the elder Whitfields."

"I can see why," Tamara said softly. "Where's the wedding going to be held?"

"Right here in Harlem. To be exact, in East Harlem. Faith and Ethan McMillan are hosting it at their brownstone. Tessa, she's the wedding planner, is sending out invitations tomorrow. Nayo, are you going to be in town that weekend?" Ava asked.

Nayo felt two pairs of eyes fixed on her and looking for an answer. Had Ava assumed that because Ivan received an invitation he would automatically take her with him? She returned to Beaver Run to visit with her family every Christmas and every other Thanksgiving. This year she planned to share Thanksgiving dinner with Geoff and his family.

"Yes, I'll be here."

Tamara pressed her palms together. "Good. You'll

get to see up close and personal a Signature Bridals wedding."

Nayo bit her lip to keep from telling Tamara that she was making too many assumptions. She may have slept with Ivan, but they were *not* a couple. She was no more committed to him than he was to her. One thing she did know, and that was she couldn't sleep with him *and* another man at the same time.

She turned her attention back to cutting and dicing ingredients for the gumbo. Soon the kitchen was filled with the delicious aroma of sautéing celery, onions, peppers, okra, oregano, thyme and bay leaves.

Tamara stood at the stove beside her browning diced onions, cubed smoked turkey and minced garlic in a Dutch oven for the collard greens. The differing smells were incredibly tantalizing.

Ivan returned with the filé powder. He threw it on the table, then ran to the rear of the house to get back to his football game.

Ivan, carrying Nayo's camera equipment, followed her up the three flights of stairs to her apartment. He'd tried convincing her to spend another night at his house, but she'd refused, claiming she had to get up early to print out the photographs he'd chosen, mat them, then take them for framing.

As soon as he stepped off the stair onto the landing, a streak of blue-gray darted past his feet. "What the…"

His voice trailed off when he saw the cat winding its way around Nayo's legs. He assumed the cat had come from the neighboring apartment. The door was ajar and a television could be heard through the opening.

Nayo unlocked the door to her apartment, and the British shorthair kitten scooted inside. "That was Colin," she said, smiling. "He's one of the males in my life."

Ivan forced a smile he didn't feel. He would've preferred Nayo to say the kitten was the *only* other male in her life, not just one of them.

"Is he named for Colin Powell?"

Nayo tossed her keys on the table near the door. "No. Mrs. Anderson named him after Colin Firth."

"Who's he?"

"A British actor. He played Mr. Darcy in the television production of *Pride and Prejudice*." She gestured to the closet. "You can put the bag right there."

Ivan lifted his broad shoulders in a gesture that said he couldn't care less who Colin Firth was. What he wanted was to spend more time with Nayo. They'd spent most of the afternoon and evening at Kyle's house, but most of that time he'd been watching two football games. During the second game's halftime, he'd apologized for neglecting her. Nayo shrugged off his apology, saying she was enjoying herself cooking and talking with Tamara and Ava.

And when he'd observed the women together, he

realized they were the quintessential football widows. They'd bonded because their men were too involved in the game to interact with them.

He'd counseled women who'd had affairs because they felt unappreciated and neglected by their sports-obsessed husbands or partners. Unfortunately when their indiscretion was uncovered, the men never accepted blame. One man told him at least his wife knew where he was when he wasn't with her: in front of a television at home or in a sports bar.

After he'd gathered and analyzed the data on women who cheat, he discovered most of them shared similar attributes: all were mothers, married for a minimum of five years, three worked at home and seven worked outside the home, which provided them ready access to other men. Closer analysis revealed none had careers, not even the women who'd graduated from college.

This was how his patients in the research study differed from Nayo, Tamara and Ava. Nayo was making a name for herself as a photographer, Tamara was a medical doctor and Ava was a licensed social worker. Not once had the three complained they were being ignored. They'd hung out in the kitchen, talking, cooking and bonding.

Fortunately Ivan hadn't become a sports junkie. He knew some men who were rabid fans of baseball, football, boxing, basketball *and* hockey. Whereas baseball and football were enough to feed his sports appetite.

Nayo slipped out of her coat and hung it in the closet. She turned to find Ivan watching her. "I'm going to try to get your framed photographs back to you before the end of the week."

He took a step, closing the distance between them. "There's no rush."

Tilting her head, Nayo regarded the brooding expression on the face of the man, a stranger, who made her want him when she hadn't wanted to, when she couldn't afford to let her heart rule her head.

In the past, because of her unorthodox lifestyle, she'd believed there was no room in her life for romance. But that changed when she found an apartment, secured a position with the auction house and held her first photographic exhibition. Her professional life was on track, and she had a lover for the first time in years. In other words, life was beautiful, and would remain beautiful only if she was able to balance her personal and professional life.

Ivan had asked her to spend another night with him when she'd already given him Friday and Saturday night. When she declined his offer, he hadn't said anything because he didn't *have* to say anything. His expression said it all: he was upset.

Nayo knew why she'd been reluctant to get involved with a man when she watched his dark eyes change, hardness replacing the tenderness that had been there seconds before.

Resting her hands on his chest, she leaned into him. "I'll call you."

Ivan buried his face between her scented neck and shoulder. "I'll call you back."

She smiled. "I'll miss you." Her voice was muffled in his sweater.

"I'll miss you, too."

Easing back, Nayo gazed up at Ivan "Good night."

His head came down and he gave her a kiss that brought tears to her eyes and left her feeling weak and confused. What, she wondered, was Ivan doing to her? Was he using silent persuasion to wear her down till she was helpless to resist him and his lovemaking?

Somewhere, somehow she found the strength to end the kiss. "Go home, Ivan."

A knowing smile tilted the corners of his mouth as if he knew exactly what he was doing and what she was feeling.

"Good night, doll face."

Nayo walked him to the door as Colin rubbed against her legs. Bending over, she picked up the kitten, cradling him to her chest as she watched Ivan descend the staircase. She waited and watched until he disappeared from her line of vision. Carrying the feline, she pushed open her neighbor's door and placed him inside, closing the self-locking door behind her.

Nayo then returned to her apartment, closed and locked the door, sliding the safety chain in place. She planned to brush her teeth, shower and go directly to bed. Dyana had given her Monday off, but that didn't mean she would have a day of rest.

Her to-do list also included developing the pictures she'd taken of Ivan and meeting with Ava and Tamara to show them her portfolio. She'd promised the two women she would prepare a light dinner, rather than go to a restaurant, but they overruled her, saying they would bring dinner.

Nayo went through the ritual of turning on the radio before she walked into the bathroom. She stripped off her clothes, leaving them in a large wicker basket that served as a clothes hamper. Twenty minutes later she flipped the switch for the track lights and slipped into bed.

Exactly forty minutes after she pushed the snooze button on the radio, it shut off. Tonight she'd fallen asleep before the music stopped.

Nayo sat at a small, round table with a man whose framing shop had occupied the same site for more than thirty years. She'd cropped the photographs that would hang on the walls in Ivan's house and printed them on the highest-quality photographic paper.

A heavily veined hand dotted with age spots turned over a matted photo to read the notation on the Post-it. "Do you want metal or wood for this one?"

"I'd like wood, please."

She'd met Sid Wagner her first year in college. Whenever she entered his tiny shop in Alphabet City, tucked between a secondhand bookstore and a tailor, she felt like a kid in a candy store. He'd established a reputation for stretching and framing works of needlepoint, but when art students discovered he offered them deep discounts, they flocked to his shop.

Nayo pointed to a color chart. "I'd like this color brown for the shadow boxes."

Sid, always cognizant of his thinning hair, patted his comb-over. "I don't have that color in stock. I'll have to order it, Nola."

Nayo had stopped correcting his pronunciation of her name. Sidney had continued to call her Nola even though she'd told him her name was pronounced *Nawyo* and was Yoruba for "our joy."

"How long do you think that's going to take?" She wanted to frame all of Ivan's photographs so they could be hung before the magazine photographer scheduled a date for shooting the layout.

Pursing his thin lips, Sid squinted at a wall calendar. "If I call it in today, then I should have it back, say, in a week." Aging blue eyes met a pair of glowing dark brown ones. "These photographs are very good, Nola. Some of the finest I've seen in a very long time."

"Thank you." Nayo knew that a compliment from the professional framer was comparable to winning a Pulitzer for photography.

"Who's the lucky person?"

"It's for someone who just finished decorating their home and needs wall hangings."

"I hope she knows what she's getting."

Nayo wanted to tell him that *she* was a *he*. "She does," she said, not bothering to correct him. Not that it would make a difference.

She'd quoted a figure for the photos and Ivan hadn't blinked when he wrote the check. He'd also signed the release for the photos she planned to eventually include in her book. They'd concluded all business before sleeping together.

Her body reacted crazily whenever she recalled sleeping with Ivan. They'd made love the first time on Saturday afternoon, and again early Sunday morning before sharing a shower. She hadn't packed her hairdryer or curling brush, and so a regular brush and a dab of gel tamed her curly hair.

Nayo checked her watch. She had less than an hour to get back to Harlem before Ava and Tamara arrived. "Do you have any botanical prints on hand?" she asked Sid. He had a small supply of prints left behind by customers who either forgot or didn't have the money to pick up their order.

"I have about a dozen exquisite Audubon reproductions. Which one do you want—birds or plants?"

"Both." They would go well with the guest bedroom's tropical decor.

It was another quarter of an hour before she selected the prints for the bedrooms, gave Sid a check for half the order, then walked outside to hail a taxi to take her uptown.

Chapter 12

Smiling, Nayo opened the door, inviting Tamara and Ava into her apartment. "Let me take your jackets."

Ava slipped off her short wool jacket, her eyes widening in surprise. "I love your apartment."

Tamara handed Nayo a shopping bag from which wafted the most delicious smells. "That's dinner. And I agree with Ava. Your place is exquisite. I've been in studio apartments that are so crowded there's no place to walk without bumping into things."

Nayo took the bag to the kitchen. "I can't stand clutter."

Ava slipped out of her boots, leaving them under the

table near the door. "I hope you don't mind if I walk around in my socks."

Nayo raised a leg, wiggling her toes in a pair of thick brown socks. "Join the club. Do you want to eat first or look at photos?"

Ava pressed two hands to her belly. "I'd rather eat first. I had to skip lunch because of a meeting outside the office."

"The bathroom is through that door," Nayo said as she gathered the coats.

Her day had begun at dawn when she dusted the apartment, set the table with place settings for three, then sat down to the task of printing photographs. Her pulse accelerated when she went through the frames she'd taken of Ivan. To say the camera loved him was an understatement.

What she'd suspected when shooting him was verified in the finished product. He had no bad side or angle. Closer inspection revealed vertical lines between his eyes whenever he smiled, and the lines bracketing his mouth were more like slashes in his lean jaw. As promised, she'd called Ivan to wish him a good day, but her call went directly to voice mail. Then she remembered he taught Monday and Wednesday mornings.

Now, she emptied the shopping bag of containers of a variety of hot and cold dishes when Ava and Tamara emerged from the bathroom. Ava wore a tailored blue pantsuit with a white silk shirt. Tamara had chosen a black slim skirt ending midcalf with a pair of riding boots and matching turtleneck sweater. Both women wore a light cover of makeup.

"Who does your hair?" Nayo asked Ava.

Ava smiled. "I do it myself."

Nayo blinked. "We have similar hair texture, yet I can't get my hair to look like yours unless I go to a salon and they set it in rollers, then blow it out."

"Do you have a flatiron?"

Nayo nodded. "I have every hair contraption known to man. I tried flatironing my hair, and it came out crazy."

"Do you flatiron it wet or dry?"

"Usually it's wet."

"Mine always comes out better if I towel-dry it first," Ava said. "After we eat I'll show you how to do it."

"Thanks."

"It's all good," Ava drawled.

"While ya'll have to wash and blow-dry hair, I have to go and get new growth touched up every six to eight weeks," Tamara said. "What ticks me off is that I have to make the next appointment before I leave the salon. The owner says it's for efficiency, while I call it a hustle."

"Where do you go?" Nayo asked.

Tamara sucked her teeth, a habit her mother detested. "It's some hoity-toity place on the Upper East Side. They claim their clients are celebrities, but I've never seen one walk through the door."

"What if you want a regular wash and set?" Ava asked.

"They'll take a walk-in or give you an appointment for the next day, but not if you need a color or straightening. The only thing that's worse is the price list. If I knew some young girl in beauty school, I'd pay her to do my hair."

"I may be able to help you out there," Ava volunteered. "I have a client who has a sister who does hair out of her apartment. The only drawback is that it's not in the best of neighborhoods."

Tamara exhaled a sigh. "There are no so-called good neighborhoods anymore."

Nayo put out a pitcher of sweet tea to go along with lentil soup, couscous salad with cherry tomatoes and bell pepper, and Mediterranean chicken prepared with a mix of such aromatic flavors as basil, garlic, olives and fennel.

She liked interacting with Ava and Tamara. Both were friendly, outgoing and totally unpretentious. Tamara disclosed she didn't wear her ring at the hospital because whenever she had to put on latex gloves, she encountered a problem, so not many of her colleagues were aware of her engagement. Ava, on the other hand, wore her ring, with its cushion-cut center diamond, proudly.

After dinner Nayo handed Tamara the photos she planned to exhibit at her next showing and include in her coffee-table book. Each photo was in a plastic sleeve.

Tamara stared at color and black-and-white photos, unable to believe what she was seeing. The images seemed to leap off the paper. "These are incredible."

Ava went completely still when she recognized the face of the man staring intently into the camera lens. "Oh—my—word!" she gasped. "I had no idea Ivan looked like this."

Leaning to her right, Tamara saw what Ava was talking about. "Sweet baby boy! When did you take this, Nayo?"

Nayo chided herself for not putting the photographs of Ivan in a separate folder. The women were staring at the one when Ivan had taken off his shirt and extended his arms above his head. The definition in his upper body was jaw-dropping spectacular.

Her cheeks burned when she remembered what had followed his uninhibited photo session. "It was this past weekend."

Tamara couldn't pull her gaze away from the expression of pure sensuality on Ivan's face. "I wonder what he was thinking about when you took this shot."

"Don't even go there," Ava crooned. "I can't believe he's been hiding all this under those Hawaiian shirts."

Nayo smiled. "It shocked me, too."

"Being a doctor, you'd think I'd be used to seeing a naked body. But looking at a specimen like Ivan

Campbell is a reminder of how perfect the body can be if it's taken care of. I can't decide whether I like him with or without his top," Tamara admitted.

Ava whistled softly. "Do you retouch your photos, Nayo?"

"Not these ones. But if I shoot weddings or take professional head shots, I usually fix the imperfections."

"Well, you've just got yourself a client," Ava declared. "Will you come to San Juan and photograph my wedding?"

"Yes." She'd checked her schedule and she was free that weekend.

"You can photograph mine, too," Tamara added.

Things were happening so quickly for Nayo that she found it hard to grasp her newfound success. Ever since she'd picked up her first camera to take a picture of her favorite doll, she'd been hooked. Twenty-five years later she'd turned her childhood passion into a career. Her first exhibition was a rousing success and the art critics were more than generous with their praise. Her photographs would appear on the glossy pages of an international, celebrated, interior-design magazine and she'd just been commissioned to photograph two Signature Bridals weddings.

It was after ten when she closed the door behind Ava and Tamara. She'd washed her hair, towel-dried it and sat, stunned, when Ava showed her how to flatiron her hair. The result was no frizzy ends. Ava also brushed her hair in a circular motion around her head, keeping it in place with large bobby pins.

The telephone rang and she went to her bedroom to answer it. "Hello." Her voice came out breathless even though she'd only had to walk a few feet from the bathroom to the bed.

"I'm sorry. I'm just returning your call."

Nayo went completely still. She heard something in Ivan's voice that hadn't been there before. "What's the matter, Ivan?"

A beat passed. "I had a patient who had an episode today."

"I know you can't discuss your patients, but if you need someone to talk to, I'm here."

Another beat. "I'll see you before eleven."

Nayo ended the call. She'd just invited a man to spend the night. But Ivan wasn't just any man. He was her lover.

Ivan fastened his mouth to Nayo's within seconds of her closing and locking the door. He needed her. For the first time in his life he needed a woman—and it wasn't for sex.

One arm went around her waist and he lifted her effortlessly off her feet, while his leather backpack slung over one shoulder slid to the floor. He carried her to the bed, easing her onto the mattress, his body following hers down.

Pain, anger and frustration merged when he took her mouth in a hungry kiss as if he wanted to devour her whole. Nayo Goddard had come to represent all that was good, all that was unencumbered by the tragic events in his past. She was a free spirit living by her own rules.

He could never predict what would come out of her mouth, never guess her next move. When they'd made love a second time on the weekend, it'd been Nayo who'd taken the initiative, giving pleasure before taking her own. She'd been selfless, and when he lay gasping for breath after the most exquisite sexual pleasure he'd ever experienced, she lay between his outstretched legs and drifted off to sleep.

"I need you, baby," he said now. "I need you so much."

Nayo heard the desperation in Ivan's voice, felt the tension in his body. "I'm here, darling. I'll always be here for you."

Ivan left the bed to take off his jacket, dropping it on a padded bench at the foot of the bed. He smiled. Tonight Nayo had pulled back the embroidered mosquito netting, tying it to the decoratively carved posts.

His gaze met and fused with hers as he took off his clothes, one garment at a time, seemingly in slow motion. His gaze slid lower to her chest. An oversize white T-shirt, doubling as a nightshirt, failed to conceal the outline of her firm breasts.

Nayo rose to her knees and held out her hand. "Come."

Ivan joined her on the bed and she moved into his embrace. They held each other, hearts keeping perfect syncopation. "A patient killed someone today," he said quietly.

"Oh, no," she whispered.

"He'd returned from his second deployment in Iraq when he began showing signs of post-traumatic stress. He refused to be treated at the VA hospital, so he was referred to me. A psychiatrist had prescribed an anti-depressant, but he wouldn't take them. Whenever he heard a loud noise or loud voices, he'd drop to the floor in a fetal position. He got into an argument with a teenage boy who wouldn't turn down his music. When the police arrived, they were met with a scene that looked like the inside of a slaughterhouse. He'd used a hunting knife in an attempt to decapitate the teen."

Nayo swallowed the bile rising in the back of her throat. "Where is he, Ivan?"

"He's in the psych ward at Bellevue Hospital."

She closed her eyes. "What's going to happen to him?"

"I don't know, baby. I'll probably be called to testify at his trial as to his mental state."

"Did you get a chance to talk to him?"

Ivan nodded. "Yes."

There was a pregnant silence as he recalled the blank look in his patient's eyes when he talked about how he couldn't take loud noises. That the music sounded like grenades and he had to stop it.

"I'm sorry to drop this on you, but it's not every day I see what had been a highly functioning young man with his whole life ahead him lose his grip on reality because he had to perform unspeakable acts under the guise of war."

Nayo wrapped her arms around Ivan's head, pulling his face to her breasts. "Don't apologize, darling. A friend is not a friend if you can't come to them when you need to talk."

"I'd like to believe we're more than friends, doll face."

She smiled. "Well, close friends."

"I'd say we're closer than close."

"How close, Ivan?"

His right hand caressed her leg, then moved between her thighs. "This close," he whispered, cupping her furred mound.

Nayo couldn't control the ripple of desire shooting through her body. Her breath was coming in quick pants as his fingers worked their magic. "Please," she begged shamelessly. She was on fire and only Ivan could extinguish it.

Reaching down, Ivan pulled the T-shirt up and over Nayo's head. Then he fastened his mouth to hers and eased her back to the mound of pillows. Slowly, meticulously, his tongue flicked out as he tasted her throat. Moving lower, he licked her breasts as if they were a sweet, chocolate confection. A low moan followed his downward journey when his tongue dipped into the indentation of her belly button.

"Don't!" he whispered hoarsely when Nayo arched off the mattress in an attempt to escape his rapacious tongue. "Let me taste you."

Nayo was afraid, afraid of the strange sensations holding her prisoner to a desire she'd never experienced. "I can't let you do that," she gasped.

Resting a hand on her flat belly, Ivan held her fast. "Yes, you can, baby."

He'd come to Nayo seeking succor from the horror of the crime scene, then witnessing the unrepentant expression in his patient's eyes when he believed he hadn't done anything wrong. Ivan hadn't come to make love, and hadn't brought protection.

Nayo had been emphatic when she told him she wasn't ready for marriage or motherhood. After meeting and sleeping with her, he'd rethought his decision to remain a bachelor. He still hadn't ascertained whether his ambivalence had something to do with the woman in whose bed he lay now or seeing the transformation in his friends, who'd committed to spending their lives with the women they loved.

Sliding down Nayo's scented body, he pressed his face to the soft down and inhaled the essence of her femininity. He placed tiny kisses along the inside of her thighs until they parted and gave him the access he sought; then he buried his face in her sex and drank deeply.

Nayo felt her heart stop, then start up again when she felt the tiny flutters in her body. Ivan's mouth was doing things to her that left her gasping and praying for it to never end. But he was relentless, his tongue and teeth tasting and nipping her sensitized flesh until she felt as if she were coming out of her skin.

Ivan made love to Nayo with his mouth when he really wanted to be inside her. He wanted to experience when they ceased to be separate entities, with passion and desire merging and lifting them outside themselves in a shared moment of unbridled ecstasy. He wanted to release his passion in her warm, throbbing flesh, then wait for the runaway beating of their hearts to return to normal.

He plunged his tongue into her vagina over and over, simulating his penis sliding in and out of her body. He felt her go completely still for several seconds, then buck wildly as he cradled her hips. At last, in a moment of madness, he pulled his mouth away and lay on top of her as his passion erupted, spilling over her belly. *I love you.* The silent declaration reverberated in his head and filled his heart to the point of bursting.

Tears spilled down Nayo's cheeks, disappearing into the pillow under her head as waves of lingering passion throbbed through her body. Even if she'd fantasized, she couldn't have imagined a deeper ecstasy, a more intense, explosive pleasure.

"Ivan?" Her voice was barely a whisper.

"Yes, baby."

"You're crushing me."

Ivan didn't know where he got the energy, but he rolled off her and onto his side. A smile flitted across his face when Nayo looped an arm over his waist and pressed her chest to his back. They lay together, spoon-like, until sleep overtook them.

He awoke later, slipped out of bed to turn off the floor lamp, then returned to the warmth of the bed and the body he'd come to crave like an addictive drug.

Chapter 13

Nayo stepped back to survey her handiwork. She smiled. She'd personally hung the pictures in Ivan's apartment. He'd wanted to pay someone to do it, but she'd overruled him.

Sid had told her that he'd have her framing order complete in about a week, but he was proved wrong when the factory he'd ordered the materials from had burned to the ground and he'd had to use an alternative supplier. Sid had then offered to take an additional ten percent off the total and promised to have the completed photos and prints delivered to Ivan's brownstone—in the past Nayo had always had to pick up her order.

And so today Sid had come through. It was the day

before Thanksgiving and she'd spent all morning and part of the afternoon hanging pictures.

The heat of Ivan's body seeped into her as he pressed his chest to her back. She shivered when he planted a kiss on the nape of her neck.

"It looks nice."

Folding her arms under her breasts, she angled her head. It'd taken hours of measuring to determine where to position the prints in the many rooms. She'd decided to add a series of prints along the hallway outside the bedrooms, too.

"I have to agree with you. What time are you expecting Carla?"

Ivan glanced at his watch. "She should be here any minute."

"I hope you're ready, because once your apartment is featured in the magazine, you're going to get a lot of attention from all the single ladies."

He kissed the nape of her neck. Ivan wasn't certain whether he liked Nayo's new sleek hairstyle. He knew she looked different but hadn't figured it out until he realized he missed seeing the shiny black curls.

"I have all the attention I can handle with *this* single lady. Besides, my name and address will not appear in the magazine."

"Have you ever considered marriage?"

Ivan froze. Nayo was asking the question his relatives never failed to ask him whenever they got together. "No."

Nayo turned to face him. She tried reading his impassive expression and failed. It was as if he'd pulled down a shade to conceal his innermost feelings. "You have to know you're what every together sister is looking for in a man. It's too bad you've taken yourself off the market."

Ivan blinked once. "Are you asking for yourself, or have you become an advocate for sisters looking for a man? If you are, then I'm not interested or available."

Nayo recoiled as if he'd struck her across the face. "What a cruel thing to say to me."

"Since when is being honest cruel, Nayo?"

She struggled to control her rising temper. "I'm not asking for myself or anyone else. And you know my views on marriage. I—" Her cell phone rang, stopping her verbal assault. Taking the tiny instrument out of the back pocket of her jeans, she stared at the display. It was Geoff.

She flipped the top. "Hi."

"Are we still on for tomorrow?"

"Yes, we're still on. What time do you want me to come?"

"I'll pick you up around two."

Nayo saw Ivan watching her intently, so she walked out of the living room to the alcove, where a fire blazed in the fireplace. "You don't have to pick me up. I can take a cab."

"Mother arranged for her driver to pick you up and take you back home."

Nayo wanted to ask Geoff if he always did what Mother said, but held her tongue. The fact that Geoffrey Magnus was still a mama's boy grated on her nerves. Although he'd come into his trust fund, he hadn't moved out of the house where he'd grown up. And for Nayo, moving into an apartment in the same building where your parents lived did not constitute being on your own.

"I'll be ready at two."

"I'll see you tomorrow."

"Tomorrow," she repeated.

Returning the cell to her jeans pocket, she walked back into the living room to discover that Ivan had removed the leveler, step stool and hammer she'd used to hang the photos. She left the living room and found him in the kitchen.

"I'm leaving now," she said.

His eyes widened. "Aren't you going to stay to see Carla's reaction?"

Nayo shook her head. "No. You can tell me when I see you Saturday."

Simone Whitfield-Madison had sent invitations to select family members and friends to witness her repeating her vows to her husband of three months. The ceremony that was scheduled for four, with a reception dinner immediately following the exchange of vows, was to be held in her cousin's East Harlem brownstone.

Ivan had asked if she would accompany him, and

Nayo hadn't hesitated because she was anxious to meet the celebrated owners of Signature Bridals before going to Puerto Rico for Ava and Kyle's beachfront wedding.

"I'd like you to stay. Please."

She blew out a breath. "Okay."

Ivan chided himself for pleading and for Nayo making it sound as if she were doing him a favor. He didn't know what it was, but he was beginning to feel as if they were drifting apart. It began when Nayo complained about not feeling well. Days later she came down with a cold that left her coughing, sneezing and sniffing for a week.

He'd gone to her apartment to offer her some TLC, but she refused to open the door to him, and whenever he called, she couldn't talk because it precipitated a coughing jag. Once she recovered and he went to see her, Ivan couldn't believe he was looking at the same woman. Her weight loss was frightening, and he'd embarked on a campaign to make certain she ate a minimum of three meals each day. She'd regained some weight, at least enough to fill out what had been petite curves.

Closing the distance between them, he gathered her in a protective embrace. "Why won't you come with me tomorrow?"

Nayo rested her cheek on his chest, listening to the steady strong beats of his heart. "I'd already made plans."

"Can't you back out?"

Tilting her chin, she glared at Ivan. "No! Even if I could, I wouldn't."

He flashed a sensual smile. "You can't blame a brother for trying."

She returned his smile. "Yes, I can, when that brother is scheming and scamming on a sister."

"But when the sister looks like you, then you can't blame a brother for at least trying."

"Dial down the bull, Ivan."

His eyebrows shot up. "Is that what you—" The chiming of the doorbell interrupted what he planned to say. Ivan grimaced at the same time he smothered a savage expletive.

"I heard that," Nayo called as he walked out of the kitchen.

Ivan continued walking. If the doorbell hadn't rung, he would've told Nayo that he knew she was spending Thanksgiving with Geoff, that he was not only jealous of the man, but also jealous of their easygoing relationship.

Whenever Geoff called Nayo, he noticed the change in her voice, how her voice grew softer, more sensual. Another thing he noticed, particularly at the Halloween party, which now seemed eons ago, was how Geoff looked at her. As a man he recognized lust in another man's eyes.

Geoffrey Magnus not only wanted Nayo Goddard in his bed, he wanted her in his life. He wanted what Ivan wanted, and Ivan was certain Geoff had made his intentions known in very few words.

Meanwhile he himself had become an expert in denial. Unofficially he and Nayo had become a couple. Whenever he got together with Kyle and Duncan and their fiancées, Nayo was there with him. When it was his turn to host Sunday afternoon or evening football at his home, Nayo was there with him. Each and every time he and Nayo were together it was as a couple, a couple among other couples.

Suddenly it hit him as he pressed a button on the intercom. How could he not have seen it before? He and Nayo went out together, but always in the company of others. Both had fairly busy schedules, but not so busy he couldn't find time to court her.

"Yes?" he said into the speaker.

"It's Carla."

Ivan opened the door and Carla Harris swept into the apartment with the aplomb of a model strutting down the runway. She spun around, a black wool cape fluttering out around her body like Batman's cape. She stopped twirling long enough to offer him an air kiss.

"Ivan. Darling. You look simply gorgeous." How, she mused, could one man look so utterly delicious in a pair of jeans, T-shirt and low-heeled boots?

He gazed at her under lowered lids. "Thank you, Carla."

She stared at him through the lenses of her red glasses. "Are you all right?"

Ivan's impassive expression did not change. "I'm fine, thank you."

"My, my, my," she said. "Aren't *we* formal today?"

Carla saw movement out the corner of her eye, and she recognized the young woman joining her and Ivan. "It's nice to see you again, Nayo."

Nayo extended her hand. "How have you been, Carla?"

"Business is good." She took the proffered hand. "I am so certain that after the layout of Ivan's home appears in AD, I'll have business coming out the yin-yang." Carla winked at the photographer who went by only one name. "I heard your first showing almost sold out."

Nayo knew Carla could've only gotten that information from Geoff, and she planned to talk to him about talking about *her* business. "Thankfully, it was quite successful."

Carla waved a hand. "You're much too modest, Nayo." She turned and smiled at Ivan. "Please show me what you've put on your walls."

Nayo's eyes met Ivan's. "I'll be in the kitchen."

Carla watched Ivan staring at Nayo's retreating figure. She'd seen that look enough times to know when a man was enchanted by a woman. For Ivan that woman happened to be a very talented photographer who was making a name for herself in the art world.

She followed Ivan in and out of rooms, pausing to study the framed and matted photos and prints. What he'd selected to grace the walls of his home was nothing short of perfection, black-and-white photographs and colorful prints complemented the personality of the rooms in which they hung.

"Bravo, Ivan," she said, applauding softly. "You have chosen well." Carla retrieved her BlackBerry from her tote, accessing her calendar. "I have several dates the photographer is available to shoot the layout. You're going to have to let me know when you will be available."

"E-mail me the dates."

She punched several keys. "I just did. Someone at the magazine will send you a packet outlining the terms and conditions of the layout. It will look more daunting than it actually is, so I suggest you give it to your lawyer to look over before you sign and return it."

Ivan nodded. He would give it to Kyle, who handled all his legal business. "Okay."

Carla patted his shoulder. "You did well, Ivan. In fact, you did better than I would've done. I'm going to let you get to your business with Nayo. If I don't see you before the end of the year, then Merry Christmas and Happy New Year."

Leaning over, Ivan kissed her cheek. "Same to you." He escorted Carla to the door, waiting until he saw her get into her car before he closed the door. He found

Nayo in the kitchen sitting on a tall stool at the cooking island, sipping from a mug.

Ivan had tried to convince Nayo to come with him to his sister's house in Staten Island for Thanksgiving dinner. He usually shared the holiday with his parents, but this year Roberta had volunteered to do the cooking.

Roberta and her orthodontist husband had recently moved into a larger house, because after eleven years of marriage they'd decided to have another child. Ivan didn't understand why it'd taken them almost ten years to elect to do so. Whenever he asked his sister why she hadn't given him another niece or nephew, her comeback was that she was waiting for him to give *her* a niece or nephew. Ivan knew that wasn't going to happen. If he was unable to commit to one woman, he would never father a child.

He'd seen firsthand the emotional turmoil not having a father caused in a child's life. Thankfully his father had been there for him. Felton Campbell was a simple man who'd dropped out of college to go to work to help support his family when his own father was killed in a hit-and-run. He worked as a hospital orderly for thirty years, then retired and enrolled in college as a part-time student, eventually earning a long-awaited liberal arts degree.

Nayo shifted on the stool, glancing over her shoulder when Ivan walked into the kitchen. "How did it go?"

Ivan angled his head and smiled. "She loved them."

"Good." Nayo slid off the stool. "I really have to go home now."

"Would you like to go to the movies?"

She looked at Ivan, her expression registering shock. "Tonight?"

"Yes, tonight."

Her gaze narrowed. "Why?"

"Why," he repeated, "because we hardly do anything together."

Nayo studied Ivan's lean face, silently admiring his exquisite bone structure. "We do everything together," she argued softly.

Reaching for the mug, he eased it from her grip, setting it on the countertop. "Whenever we do anything, it's always with Kyle, Duncan and their fiancées."

"I thought you enjoyed hanging out with them."

"I do. But I'd like to spend more time with you—alone."

"Why do you want to change things, Ivan? I enjoy you. I hope you enjoy me. And there's no doubt we enjoy each other's friends."

"Speak for yourself, doll face."

Nayo rolled her eyes at the same time as she shook her head. "Why don't you like Geoff?"

"Did I mention his name?"

"You didn't have to, Ivan. Every time he calls me you seem to catch an attitude. Not only are we friends, but Geoff and I are colleagues."

"A colleague who wants to…"

"What, Ivan?" she asked when he didn't finish his statement.

"You know what he wants, Nayo."

"No, I don't. You tell me."

Ivan stared at Nayo, not wanting to argue with her. What he enjoyed more was kissing her and making love with her. And it'd been weeks since they'd gone to bed together. Once she recovered from the cold, she told him she was on her menses. He'd canceled evening hours tonight because he'd learned from past experience that patients tended to skip their sessions the day before a holiday.

"Come. I'll take you home."

Ivan reached for her jacket off the back of the stool, then held it while Nayo slipped her arms into the sleeves. He picked up his own jacket and keys, which he'd left on a low stool near the entrance to the kitchen.

They walked out of the brownstone and when they reached the corner, Ivan took Nayo's hand. It was a cold, crisp, late-November day. The local supermarket was crowded with shoppers picking up last-minute items for their Thanksgiving dinner.

"You don't have to walk me up," Nayo said to Ivan as they neared her apartment building.

"Please don't tell me what I *don't* have to do, Nayo. I'm walking you upstairs."

There were times when Nayo found Ivan to be the

most stubborn, exasperating man she'd ever met. Once he set his mind to something, it was almost impossible to get him to change it. The first time she accused him of not being flexible, not wanting to compromise, he'd glared at her, obviously hoping she would cave in under his intimidation. She didn't, and the evening ended in an impasse with her asking him to take her home.

Tossing her keys at him, she waited for him to unlock the door leading into the vestibule. She preceded Ivan up the staircase, feeling the heat of his gaze on her back. Mrs. Anderson was on the upper landing, trying to coax Colin back into her apartment. When the feline spied Nayo, he scooted back into his apartment and her neighbor quickly closed the door. Colin had taken to running off as soon as his owner opened the door. One day the building superintendent found him curled up next to the radiator near the door that led to the basement.

Ivan unlocked the door to Nayo's apartment. Heat and the soft glow from a floor lamp enveloped him when he walked in. He handed Nayo her keys. "I'll pick you up at three-thirty on Saturday for the wedding."

She smiled. "I'll be ready." They only had to walk one block to the McMillans'.

Ivan angled his head and brushed his mouth over Nayo's. "Enjoy your Thanksgiving."

"You, too. Good night, Ivan."

He winked at her. "Good night, doll face."

Chapter 14

Miriam Magnus, or Mimi as she was affectionately called by her friends, rested a hand on Nayo's back. "May I please see you alone for a moment?"

Nayo looked at the tall, slender woman with her peaches-and-cream complexion, light gray eyes and flaxen hair. "Yes. Of course."

She followed Geoff's mother to a small room off the living room where Mimi usually received and entertained friends. "Please sit down, Nayo."

Perched on the edge of a near-perfect reproduction of a Queen Anne chair, Nayo decided to take the initiative, saying, "Why do want to see me?"

Mimi fingered the double strand of priceless pearls around her smooth neck. She studied Nayo Goddard, seeing why her son was so taken with her. She was petite, her rounded face doll-like, and she was talented—Mimi had seen the photographs Geoff had set up for her showing. Mimi smiled upon recognizing the designer shoes on Nayo's feet. With her black wool pantsuit and white silk blouse, Nayo reminded her of herself when she was younger.

"I'd like to talk to you about your relationship with my son."

Nayo's expression did not change, despite the knot clenching and unclenching in the pit of her stomach. "Geoff and I don't have a relationship."

Mimi lifted her eyebrows. "What is it you do have?"

"We're friends, Mrs. Magnus."

"Friends?" the older woman repeated. "How long have you and Geoffrey been friends?"

"Ten years."

Crossing her legs at the ankles, Mimi leaned forward. "Isn't that long enough for you and Geoffrey to stop being friends, Nayo? How long are you going to continue to lead him on?"

Nayo wanted to scream at the presumptuous woman and slap the hell out of Geoff for putting her in this position. "I don't know what your son told you, but there was nothing and never will be anything other than respect and friendship between Geoff and me."

"Are you aware that my son is in love with you?"

"And I'm in love with another man."

Nayo couldn't believe the words that had come out of her mouth. She'd confessed to Miriam Magnus that she was in love, without disclosing Ivan's name. The confession shocked her as much as it shocked Geoff's mother, who sat with a stunned expression freezing her patrician features.

"Have you told Geoffrey?" Mimi asked when she recovered her voice.

"No," Nayo said truthfully. "Geoff and I don't discuss our private lives. Are you aware, Mrs. Magnus, that Geoff does date other women?"

Mimi nodded. "Women who are out to use him."

"What makes you think I won't use him?"

"I'm praying you won't."

"Did Geoff ask you to talk to me?"

Mimi shook her head. "No. He wouldn't have the nerve."

"I don't want to sound disrespectful, but you have a lot of nerve to question me about your son, who happens to be a thirty-year-old man who, I can assure you, doesn't have a problem getting a woman."

"It is not about a woman, Nayo. This is about *you.*"

"I'm not going to allow it to be all about me. Geoff and I are friends and that's all we'll ever be. However, if you decide to interfere again, as you're doing now, then I'll have no other recourse but to end that friendship. You have a choice, Mrs. Magnus."

Rising to her feet, Nayo walked away from the woman and her shocking attempt to play Cupid for a man who wasn't shy about vocalizing what he liked or didn't like. That was one of the reasons she appreciated Geoff.

He hadn't wanted her to move out of his family's Greenwich Village town house when she told him that she'd found and signed a lease for her East Harlem studio apartment.

He, in a moment of weakness when he'd had too much to drink, had professed to be in love with her. When Nayo confronted him once he was sober, Geoff hadn't tried to deny his feelings. He said he was in love with her and wanted to marry her.

The intensity of his emotions had taken her aback. To cope with his new revelation, Nayo had stopped being as available to him. She reduced the number of times they had dinner together from several times a week to once or twice a month. It wasn't easy for either, but their dependence on each other decelerated until when they did spend time together, it was quality time.

Mimi had underestimated Nayo Goddard. She'd asked to speak to the younger woman, hoping her plea would jolt Nayo into seeing what was right in front of her. Mimi knew better than anyone that her son could marry someone within the social circle that had been established for him, a privileged, rapidly shrinking circle where he could marry a young woman who complemented him in every way. However, he'd chosen to fall in love with someone outside the circle, a young woman from a little town in upstate New York that barely made the map.

She didn't blame her son for his obsession with Nayo Goddard, but she did blame Nayo for permitting Geoffrey to believe they would eventually share a future. Nayo had admitted she was in love with another man, but had she verbalized that to her poor little lovesick son?

Mimi doubted it, or else Geoffrey wouldn't have gone on and on about looking forward to seeing Nayo at dinner. When she'd asked Geoffrey the last time he and Nayo had gotten together, his response was "just before Halloween." It'd been more than a month since her son had seen his best friend, and Mimi wasn't going to permit him to mope around as if he'd *lost* his best friend. When she asked him about his feelings for Nayo, he hadn't hesitated. He revealed he was in love with Nayo and wanted to marry her.

Mimi had believed if she were going to have one child, it should've been a girl. However, selecting the sex of her child was something beyond her control. She had to deal with a son who'd become physically and emotionally like her father.

Her thoughts returned to Nayo, who hadn't challenged her but stood her ground. "I promise not to interfere."

Nayo smiled. "Thank you."

"What we've discussed will not go any further than this room."

"You have my word on that, Mrs. Magnus."

The two women stood up and Nayo walked out, Miriam Magnus following a minute later. She spied Geoff talking to a young woman who'd occasionally stopped by the gallery. His face was suffused with color and it was apparent he'd either had too much to drink or was excited by something the woman had said.

Nayo resented Mrs. Magnus's trying to set her up with her son. If she knew what Nayo knew about her son, she would butt out of his personal life. Geoffrey Magnus was the complete package for some woman. That woman did not happen to be Nayo Goddard.

Geoff spied Nayo, excused himself and went over to where she stood looking totally bored as his aunt, gesturing wildly, talked. The half-dozen diamond bracelets on her chubby wrists sparkled under the brilliance of an overhead chandelier, but didn't move. He'd cautioned his aunt that if she didn't lose weight, they would be forced to cut her precious and priceless bracelets off her wrist.

Nayo smiled at his approach. He slipped an arm around her waist. "Excuse me, Aunt Jane, but I must see that Nayo gets something to drink." Sotto voce, he said, "You looked as if you needed rescuing."

"I did, thank you. I think this is the umpteenth time your aunt told me how she met your uncle while on holiday in Europe."

Geoff signaled for the bartender to give him a glass of white wine. "She's told that story so many times she's beginning to believe it herself."

Nayo stared at Geoff. He'd cut his hair, and the cropped locks made him appear older than he had with a mass of curls falling around his face. He would go another year without cutting it, then the cycle would begin again.

She'd always found him quite attractive, but there was something about Geoffrey Magnus that wouldn't permit Nayo to see him as more than a friend. What had begun as a platonic relationship had continued through the years.

Their relationship was the complete opposite of the one she had with Ivan. A week after meeting Ivan Campbell, she'd shared his bed. She'd waited for the guilt that never came from sleeping with a man she barely knew.

Geoff handed her a glass of chilled merlot. "Thank you."

"I saw you with my mother. Is everything all right between the two of you?"

Nayo swallowed the icy liquid, savoring the taste of the wine on her tongue. "Everything is wonderful,

Geoff." She gave him a too-bright smile over the rim of her glass. "I saw you with Bethany. Is everything okay between the two of you?"

"We're good," Geoff confirmed. "I invited her to join us because she didn't want to go to Texas with her folks who went there to visit their grandchildren."

"I like her, Geoff."

His eyebrows lifted. "You do?"

"Yes," she said truthfully. Bethany Lawry was a lawyer who'd become an avid collector of antique paperweights. She stopped by Dyana Ryker's auction house on an average of twice a month to check out the inventory, and if she found anything that resembled a paperweight, the checkbook came out and the check was written and pushed across the counter before the ink dried from her antique Montblanc pen.

"I like her," Geoff stated simply.

Nayo smiled. "She's lovely."

Bethany, Nayo thought, was a throwback to the girls who went to private women's colleges. She wore her dirty-blond, modified pageboy parted off-center and tucked behind one pearl-studded ear. Cashmere twin set, single strand of pearls, pencil skirt and Gucci slip-ons completed her very conservative look.

"I asked her whether she wanted to go away with me to Hawaii for Christmas, and she said she would have to let me know."

Nayo patted Geoff's shoulder, feeling the intense

heat of his flesh through the cotton shirt. "At least she didn't say no."

Geoff's eyes darkened. "You're right, Nayo. I suppose you're going home this Christmas."

"Yes, I am." She wanted to tell Geoff that Harlem, not Beaver Run, was home.

"When are you coming back?"

"I'm not sure."

"Aren't you coming back for New Year's?"

"That depends on a few of my friends. We still haven't decided where we want to celebrate New Year's Eve."

Ava had told her that Kyle, Ivan and Duncan were talking about hosting a small gathering at home, but hadn't decided at whose home. Nayo knew if Ivan volunteered to host, she would probably step in as hostess.

Nayo wasn't certain when her relationship with Ivan had changed, but it had. And the change had taken place in bed. Their lovemaking had escalated from a relaxed, leisurely coming together to a frantic coupling that made her feel as if it would be their last time together. Instead of falling into the sated slumber reserved for lovers, she lay awake, her insides quivering from an intensity that frightened her. When she'd attempted to broach the subject with Ivan, he'd say that nothing had changed, which left her believing she was imagining something that wasn't there.

She'd blurted out to Geoff's mother that she was in love with another man, and she hadn't realized what lay in her heart until saying it aloud. She'd said she was in love with another man, yet she was unwilling to admit it to Ivan.

The Magnuses' butler walked into the living room to usher everyone into the formal dining room. It was time to sit down to a festive Thanksgiving dinner.

Ivan had just reached up to turn off the lamp when he heard the soft tapping on the door. "Come in."

His sister, bundled in a velour robe and her hair covered with a silk scarf to preserve her hairdo, stuck her head through the opening in the door. "Can I come in for a few minutes?"

Pushing into a sitting position, Ivan patted the side of the mattress. "Sure. Come sit down."

He'd given in to his older sister's pleading that he spend the night when the pleading turned into a whining he'd never been able to abide. Roberta, who would celebrate her forty-first birthday next spring, had confided to him that she suspected she was pregnant, but wanted to wait another week before making an appointment to see her ob-gyn.

"How do you like your room?" she asked, sitting on the bed.

Ivan smiled. "It's wonderful."

"Does this mean you'll come and visit more often because we now have room to put you up?"

He stared at the feminine version of his face. When

the Campbell kids were growing up, people often remarked how much they looked alike. He and Jared were identical twins, but there were times when all three kids were asked if they were identical triplets. It was Roberta who always blasted people, saying identical babies had to be the same sex.

Ivan had become the twin known for fighting, because he was the one who stepped up to defend his sister after she'd mouthed off at someone invariably older and bigger than she was. But everything changed the summer Jared died. If the two remaining Campbell children weren't in school, they could be found at home. Ivan would've been virtually a hermit if Kyle hadn't come to visit him every day.

"Yes, Bertie," he teased, using her childhood nickname.

"You seemed a little quiet tonight. What's going on with you, Ivan?"

"Nothing, Bertie."

"Hel-lo, Ivan. I'm your big sister, so I know when something's bothering you. It's a woman, isn't it?" she asked perceptively when the seconds ticked off.

"What makes you think it's a woman? It could be work-related."

"One thing I know it's not and that's work-related. You're on point when it comes to your career. But I can't say the same thing for your personal life. It's in the crapper, Ivan."

"Damn, Bertie. Do you have to be so complimentary?"

"Stop trying to avoid the issue!" she snapped angrily. Roberta's deep-set dark eyes narrowed. "Talk to me, Ivan Garner Campbell. And stop glaring at me," she warned. "You know I'm not susceptible to intimidation. Your brother-in-law learned that early on, and that's why we're still married."

"Why are you trying to get into my business, Bertie?"

"Because you *are* my business, Ivan. You're the only brother I have and I worry about you."

Ivan ran a hand over the stubble on his jaw. His sister knew exactly what to say to get him to open up. Even the most oblique reference to Jared always choked him up, leaving him aching and vulnerable. All the Campbells grieved with Jared's senseless murder, but none more than Ivan. The fissure that tore his young life apart had closed, but the scar remained.

A sadness trembled over his lips before he compressed them tightly. "You're right, Bertie. It is a woman."

He told his sister about Nayo, how they'd met and his purchasing her photographs. His gaze softened when he described her. "I'm not certain where I stand with her because she lives and plays by her own rules and expects me to follow."

Roberta's waxed eyebrows shot up. "Do you?"

Ivan looked sheepish. "Most times I do."

"What happens when you don't?"

"I end up looking like the bad guy."

"There is something called compromise."

"I know," he agreed, "but most times I find myself not following the advice I give my patients."

"You can't base your relationship on a patient-treatment plan. Short- and long-terms goals usually don't work in affairs of the heart."

"Tell me about it," he mumbled.

"No, *you* tell me about it," the high school guidance counselor countered. "And you *can* leave out the intimate details."

Roberta listened intently, recognizing a passion in her brother's voice that she found shocking and endearing. It was apparent that Ivan Campbell was in love with his photographer girlfriend.

"Are you certain you're not identifying with Kyle and DG?"

A frown line appeared between Ivan's eyes. "What are you talking about?"

"The three of you have been inseparable since second grade. Now that your best friends are engaged, have you thought that perhaps subconsciously you also want to be engaged?"

His frown deepened. "I don't think so."

"You don't think so, or you know? The only way you're going to find out is to distance yourself from your friends. Make it a one-couple date, instead of three. The more alone time you spend with your girl-friend, the more you'll know whether what you feel for her is real or a fantasy."

Leaning forward, he pressed a kiss on Roberta's forehead. "Thanks for the advice."

Roberta patted his chest over the stark-white T-shirt. "Try to get some sleep before Ivana barges in and wakes you up."

Ivan winked at his sister. "I'm going to have something for my niece."

"What's that?"

"Lock the door on your way out."

"Do you really want me to lock it?"

"Your daughter, my niece and goddaughter, must adhere to boundaries. At nine years old, she shouldn't be allowed to invade another person's bedroom at will. She must learn to knock, then wait to be told to enter."

"You're right, Dr. Campbell."

Ivan smiled. "Get outta here and let me get some sleep so I'll have enough energy to hang out with my niece."

Roberta kissed his cheek. "Good night."

"Good night, Bertie."

Ivan watched as Roberta turned the lock on the doorknob before closing the door behind her. Then he switched off the lamp, plunging the bedroom in darkness.

When he'd maneuvered into the driveway leading to

his sister's home, he'd been overwhelmed by the grandeur of the three-story, five-bedroom, forty-five-hundred-square-foot mini-mansion in the upscale Staten Island neighborhood. Ivana had taken him on a tour of her new home, proudly pointing out the features that hadn't been in her old house. She was thrilled to have her own bathroom, and she loved it when her daddy started a fire in one of the many fireplaces.

His parents had moved into a retirement community a mile from their daughter, son-in-law and granddaughter.

The Campbells were doing well. Roberta had her growing family, his father and his mother had each other—and he was nearly forty and still had a fear of commitment.

Chapter 15

Nayo exited her apartment building in time to see Ivan striding up the sidewalk. Not waiting for him to reach her, she walked to meet him. She saw his look of surprise when his gaze lingered on her face.

"You cut your hair."

She smiled. "Instead of wash-and-blow hair, I decided to go with a wash-and-go style."

Ivan couldn't pull his gaze away from the short curls framing what he'd become to regard as the perfect face. The shorter style accentuated Nayo's eyes, eyes to which she'd expertly applied makeup: dark shadow on her lids and a raspberry shade over the brow bone and mascara that spiked her long lashes. His gaze moved lower to the matching raspberry gloss on her full, lush mouth.

"I'd kiss you, but I don't want to smear your lipstick."

Nayo looped her arm through his over the sleeve of his all-weather raincoat. "I'll let you slide if you promise to kiss me later."

Resting his free hand over the one in the crook of his elbow, Ivan led Nayo down the sidewalk to the block where Faith McMillan lived with her pilot husband. Faith, one-third owner of Signature Bridals, had set up her wedding-cake business on one floor of the brownstone.

"Your legs look fabulous in those shoes."

Pinpoints of heat stole their way across Nayo's face. It had taken her twenty minutes to decide what shoes to wear. She'd tried on more than six pairs until deciding on the silk-covered, midnight-blue stilettos. The additional four inches put the top of her head just above Ivan's shoulder.

"Thank you."

"What are you hiding under that coat?" Nayo wore a dark, fur, three-quarter-length swing coat over a dress ending at her knees.

She made an attractive moue. "You'll see."

"Is it something that will force me to act like a fool if another man looks at you?"

"If you're going to act like a fool, then you're on your own. I will not bail you out if you get arrested."

He gave her hand a gentle squeeze. "I doubt I'll get arrested."

"Why would you say that?"

"If the dude I punch out isn't related to the bride or groom, then I'll slide. The bride's husband is a U.S. Marshal, her brother-in-law is ex-NYPD and now a Kings County ADA, and don't forget I have Kyle to plead my defense."

"And what would your defense be?"

"Temporary insanity," Ivan said, deadpan.

"Who's going to determine your mental state?"

"Dr. Campbell."

"Dr. Campbell," Nayo repeated. "That's highly unethical, Ivan."

"Who's going to dispute me, doll face? I've testified in court as an expert witness when either the attorneys for the plaintiff or defendant want a professional opinion."

Ivan slowed his pace as they reached the middle of the block of brownstones, leading her up the stairs to a designer glass door. The geometric motifs reminded Nayo of the work of George Elmslie and Frank Lloyd Wright.

"I love the door," she said aloud.

Ivan rang the bell on a brass plate engraved with *Signature Cakes.* "Faith and Ethan have an incredible house."

"And you don't?"

"It's different. They have the entire building for their personal use. Signature Cakes occupies the first floor, their personal living space is on the second, and they use the third floor for entertaining." A dark-suited young man opened the door and Ivan handed him the invitation.

"May I please have your names, sir?"

"Ivan Campbell and Nayo Goddard."

The young man's face was so smooth Nayo doubted he shaved. She glanced around the vestibule. Like Ivan, the McMillans hadn't renovated, but rather restored their property.

The greeter checked their names off on a printed list. He handed Nayo a red ticket. "I'll check your coat for you, Miss Goddard."

She removed a tiny evening purse from her coat pocket before undoing the fastenings on the ranch-mink coat. Nayo shrugged it off and Ivan handed it to the man.

"You can take the elevator directly to the third floor."

Ivan stared in shock when he saw what lay under Nayo's coat: a strapless dark blue dress with a fitted bodice and revealing décolletage. If her legs were mind-boggling in the heels, then her petite body was mind-blowing in the dress.

Nayo saw the direction of Ivan's gaze. "If I hadn't gotten sick and lost a few pounds, I never would've been able to fit in this dress."

Resting his outstretched hand in the small of her back, Ivan led her past the staircase to the elevator at the end of the hallway. He didn't respond because he couldn't respond. The impact of seeing her in the revealing dress rendered him completely mute. The elevator door opened and another dark-suited young man smiled at them.

"Good afternoon, sir, miss."

"Good afternoon," Nayo and Ivan said in unison.

The doors closed as the car rose swiftly. The doors opened and they stepped out into a ballroom. Round tables, each with seating for six, a trio of strategically positioned chandeliers, a built-in bar and a dance floor created the perfect setting for formal or informal entertaining. A string quartet played softly in a corner while waiters balancing trays circulated among the small crowd, offering flutes of champagne and hot and cold hors d'oeuvres.

"This is beautiful."

Nayo couldn't disguise the awe in her voice. Teal-and-white-striped tablecloths and chairs covered in alternating colors of teal and white organza were pushed under the tables. A crystal vase of delicate white lily, muguet, narcissus and marigold served as a centerpiece for each table. The color scheme was repeated on the bridal table with its solid-teal tablecloth and chairs covered and tied back with white organza. A fire roared behind a decorative screen in a massive fireplace along one wall.

"It's incredible," Ivan said reverently.

She stared at her escort for the evening, frowning. His dark blue suit, white shirt, platinum-gray tie and Italian leather slip-ons were certain to make him a standout with the opposite sex, and she hoped she wouldn't have to go ghetto on some woman who attempted to come on to him.

Reaching for two flutes, Ivan handed one to Nayo. He leaned closer. "What are you frowning about?"

"I was just thinking about some hoochie coming on to my man."

"Who's your man?"

"You are," she said angrily.

His eyebrows rose. "Oh. I had no idea I was your man."

"Don't get it twisted, Ivan. I was under the impression we were a couple."

"*Were* or *are,* Nayo?" he asked, leaning closer.

"We are, Ivan."

He touched flutes. "Let's drink to that."

Peering over the rim of her flute, Nayo sipped the premium champagne, watching Ivan watching her. She missed him. Not because they hadn't seen each other for several days or made love in two weeks. It was more than anything physical or tangible. She and Ivan were drifting apart emotionally.

She'd tried analyzing all that had happened between them, but hadn't been able to come up with any answers. At first she thought the spark between them had dimmed because she hadn't taken the time to get to know Ivan before jumping into bed with him. But not sharing a bed for two weeks hadn't changed them so dramatically, surely, that she would feel estranged from a man with whom she was falling in love.

Wrapping her arm around his waist inside his jacket, Nayo melded her curves to his hard body. "I've missed you, darling."

Ivan angled his head, brushing his lips over hers. "I've missed you, too." He glanced over Nayo's head to see Kyle and Ava step off the elevator, followed by Duncan and Tamara. It appeared as if their women had called one another beforehand to ask what they would be wearing, because each woman had elected to wear a strapless dress. The two couples joined Nayo and Ivan. The three men bumped fists, the women exchanging air kisses.

Nayo curbed the urge to cover her chest with her hand. Kyle and Duncan were staring at her as if they'd never seen her before. Both men were dressed to the nines in tailored suits, custom-made shirts and silk ties.

"Is something wrong, gentlemen?" she asked.

"You cut your hair," Kyle said.

"You look so…different," Duncan said.

"What she looks is amazing," Ava added. Each time Nayo took a breath, a swell of breast rose and fell above the revealing neckline. "Excuse us, Ivan, but I want to introduce Nayo to Tessa and Faith."

Kyle winked at Duncan when he saw the direction of Ivan's gaze. "Don't look so worried, brother. They're going to bring her back," he teased Ivan.

"I know that, Kyle."

Duncan slapped a hand on Ivan's back. "Lighten up, brother. If I didn't know you better, I'd think you're ready to put a ring on your little lady's finger."

"That's not going to happen, DG."

"Are you still running the love-them-and-leave-them game?" Kyle asked.

Ivan shook his head. "This time it's not about me."

Kyle took a flute from a passing waiter. "If it's not you, then who is it about?"

"It's Nayo. She hasn't made it a secret that she has no interest in settling down or starting a family. She claims it would interfere with her career."

Duncan's arm settled over Ivan's shoulders. "Has she said she didn't want to get married, or that she's just not ready?"

Tilting his glass to his mouth, Ivan drained it. "Don't want or not ready, they're both the same."

"No, they aren't, and you of all people should know that, Dr. Campbell," Kyle drawled sarcastically. "You have answers for everyone else, but not for yourself. I think it's time you looked into diagnosing your own issues, brother."

Ivan knew his friends wanted the best for him. They'd always wanted the best for one another.

Whether it was personal tragedy, advancing their education, career or a relationship with a woman, the three were supportive of one another regardless of the outcome.

What Ivan had come to respect about Kyle and DG was their ability not to be judgmental. There were women he'd dated that Kyle and Duncan had never taken a liking to. The guys told him, kept their distance, and when it ended, never said *I told you so*.

He hadn't realized how much he'd tired of dating a different woman every two or three months. If the liaison lasted beyond the three-month limit, then he had to deal with extricating himself from the relationship with a minimum of drama.

"You guys are right." He extended his fist and he wasn't disappointed when Duncan grasped it, then Kyle placed his hand on Duncan's. The three held the position for several seconds before breaking.

Nayo followed Ava through a door that opened out to a hallway with restrooms for men and women, and a large, bustling kitchen from which wafted the most tantalizing aromas.

Ava stopped at a door marked Private, knocking lightly. "It's Ava," she said, identifying herself when a muffled voice called out behind the door.

The door opened and a tall, utterly beautiful woman with dark skin and short, black hair stood in the doorway. A pair of large Tahitian-pearl earrings suspended from a drop clasp of bezel-set diamonds shimmered in her pierced ears. A rose-pink, empire-waisted dress, with yards of silk making up the skirt, artfully concealed her advancing pregnancy.

"Come in, Ava. Tessa's helping Simone get into her gown."

"Faith, this is Nayo Goddard. She's going to photograph my wedding. Nayo, Faith Whitfield-McMillan, wedding-cake designer extraordinaire."

Faith rested a hand on her burgeoning belly. "It's nice meeting you, Nayo. Unfortunately I won't be able to go to Puerto Rico to watch you do your thing, because I'm due to give birth early January."

"Do you know what you're having?" Nayo asked her.

"No. Ethan and I decided we didn't want to know. Oh, here's Tessa."

Nayo turned to find Signature Bridals' wedding planner float into the room in an off-the-shoulder dress of chiffon and organza in a becoming teal blue. White feathers were pinned into the neat knot at the back of her head. Her earrings were a match for the pair in Faith's ears.

The skin around her catlike eyes crinkled when she smiled. "You must be Nayo Goddard." She offered her hand. "Tessa Whitfield-Sanborn. I know it's a mouthful, but I didn't want to drop the Whitfield."

Nayo shook her hand. "Professionally I'm known as Nayo."

Tessa sat in an armchair with a matching footstool as Faith and Ava left the room. She gestured to the love seat. "Please sit. We have a few minutes before the ceremony begins. Ava told me she saw samples of your work. She said they're extraordinary."

"They're good."

"Just good?" Tessa asked.

Nayo crossed one leg over the other. "Good enough to sell ninety-two of the 120 photos at my first exhibition."

Tessa whistled softly. "You *are* good. I work exclusively with two photographers, but both are booked for other weddings the same weekend as Ava and Kyle's. If you are available to travel to San Juan, then I'd like you to come along as a Signature Bridals' photographer."

"Will I have to sign a contract with you?"

"No. What I'll do is send you a list of events, their dates and locations, and you can let me know the dates of the events that appeal to you."

"What criteria do you use to select a photographer for a particular event?" Nayo asked.

"Only one—that you're a Signature Bridals photographer. Under normal circumstances I would ask you for a sample of your work and I'd send it to Peter Demetrious, who—"

"You know Peter Demetrious?" Nayo owned a book of photographs taken by the celebrated photographer to the stars.

Tessa smiled. "Yes. Are you familiar with his work?"

Nayo told the wedding planner about her cross-country trek. She'd been in L.A. at the time a museum hosted a Demetrious retrospective, and she was fortunate enough to be at the museum the afternoon the brilliant photographer was in attendance. Then she and Tessa discussed the controversy surrounding celebrity-stalking paparazzi, until Faith returned to inform them that the wedding was starting.

Ivan reached for Nayo's hand, finding it cold to the touch. Simone Whitfield-Madison and her husband stood facing each other as bride and groom for the second time in less than six months.

Nayo felt the heat from Ivan's gaze, but refused to look at him as she listened to the couple repeating their vows. The bride wore an ivory, peau-de-soie gown with an Alençon-lace bodice, scalloped waist and A-line skirt with a lace hem. She'd tied a teal, silk-taffeta sash around her narrow waist. Light from the chandelier caught the sparkle of canary diamonds in her ears.

Rafael Madison's voice bore a lingering trace of his Midwest roots when he promised to love and protect his bride. Nayo hadn't realized she was holding her breath when the tall, blond lawman walked down the red carpet to wait for his bride to join him. The photographer caught the look on his deeply tanned face and the depth of love in his dark blue eyes when Simone walked into the room on her father's arm. His silk tie and vest was the same teal blue as the sash around Simone's waist.

Simone handed her bouquet of white mini calla lilies cradled in hosta leaves and tied with teal satin ribbon to her sister, who was her matron of honor. Tessa was Simone's only attendant, and Micah Sanborn stood in as Rafael's best man.

There was the exchange of rings, the kiss, and then it was over. Simone Whitfield, floral designer and owner of Wildflowers and Other Treasures, was wed again, to Rafael Madison. This time the couple had their family and friends on hand to witness the union.

Chapter 16

The string quartet played through the many courses of the meal, prepared by the father and uncle of the bride. Seventy-two guests dined on minted pea soup, papaya-and-arugula salad with ginger-lemongrass vinaigrette. These were followed by lobster with vanilla-mint curry sauce, bamboo rice and baby bok choy.

For the guests who preferred organic cuisine, Harry and Malcolm Whitfield offered grass-fed, all-natural Angus beef filet, farm-raised salmon and coconut-almond Texas Gulf Coast wild shrimp served with a pineapple tartar sauce. The waitstaff took drink orders, and no wine or water glass went empty.

Nayo, who shared a table with Ivan, Kyle, Ava, Tamara and Duncan, pressed her shoulder to Ivan's. "If I eat another morsel, I'm going to come out of this dress," she whispered for his ears only.

Ivan's gaze was drawn to her chest. "You're already coming out of it."

She swiped at him with her napkin. "I'm not talking about my breasts."

Resting his hand on her back, he rubbed it in a comforting gesture. "Once dinner is over, I'd like you to save a dance for me."

"Only one dance?"

He smiled. "I'll take one here, and one at home."

"Your place or mine?"

Ivan's hand moved lower. "My place."

"If you stay at my place, I'll make breakfast."

"And if you stay at my place, I'll take you out for a gospel brunch," Ivan promised.

She smiled. "That settles it. I'll stay at your place."

A light tapping garnered everyone's attention when Micah Sanborn stood up to offer a toast to the newlyweds. The sprinkling of gray in his cropped hair added an air of elegance to the gorgeous assistant DA.

He held up a glass of champagne. "I'd like to say a few words to—"

"Since when can a lawyer say only a few words?" someone called out. Laughter followed.

Micah glared at his wife's brother. "He doesn't have

to say anything when he hands you an invoice for billable hours." Hoots and catcalls followed Micah's comeback. He held up his free hand for quiet. The laughter and twitters faded, then stopped altogether. "On a more serious note," he continued, "I'd like to offer Rafe some free advice from the inimitable Ogden Nash, and I quote, 'To keep your marriage brimming, with love in the loving cup, whenever you're wrong, admit it. Whenever you're right, shut up!'"

Malcolm Whitfield stood, smiling at his daughter and son-in-law. Simone had inherited her father's khaki coloring, curly hair and hazel eyes. "I raise my glass in a toast to the newlyweds—may you have more anniversaries than weddings."

Covering her face with a napkin, Simone laughed until tears rolled down her cheeks. It was her father who'd grumbled incessantly about her having a Vegas wedding, so incessantly that she and her husband had decided to renew their vows before their families.

The toasts were kept to a minimum, and after votives were set on each table and the lights in the chandeliers were dimmed, Rafael Madison led his bride out onto the dance floor for their first dance as husband and wife. A DJ had replaced the string quartet.

Then Simone danced with her father, and Rafael led his mother around the floor. There were gasps of surprise, because some in attendance were unaware that, despite his appearance, Rafael Madison was of mixed race.

Nayo overheard a woman at a table behind her whisper that although she wasn't into blonds, she'd make an exception in his case because the delicious-looking groom could put his shoes under her bed anytime he wanted.

The DJ spun an amazing repertoire of songs, ranging from slow jams to club favorites, and Nayo lost count and couldn't remember the faces of the men who spun her around the dance floor. She found herself back in Ivan's arms for a slow number. She rested her head on his shoulder.

"I can't remember the last time I danced this much."

Tightening his arm around her waist, Ivan pulled her closer. "Do they have hip-hop in Beaver Run?"

"You got jokes about my hometown?"

Ivan pressed his mouth to her ear. "No. I just thought with a name like Beaver Run, folks would be into country."

"We have the luxury of mixing Rascal Flatts with Kanye West, while throwing in a little JT."

"Who's JT?"

"Justin Timberlake."

Ivan smiled. Either he was getting old or he was out of the loop. He was more up on what was happening in popular culture when he'd headed the mental-health research center in D.C. than now. He taught college-level courses and had a private practice with patients who came to him exhibiting myriad psychological problems and disorders.

"Thanks for the update," he said.

"You're welcome. You need to get out more, Ivan."

He dipped Nayo, his mouth inches from hers, before he brought her up. Unknowingly, Nayo had just given him the perfect opening for courting her. "Will you help me?"

Pulling back slightly, Nayo stared up at him. "What on earth are you talking about?"

"Will you go with me if I decide to get out more?"

"Where do you want to go?"

"I'll go wherever it is *you* go," he said cryptically.

"Are you willing to give up your Sunday football get-togethers to spend your Sunday afternoons with me at museums or art galleries, which is what I usually do?"

"What else do you do?"

"I take walking tours of different neighborhoods photographing things and people I find interesting. Weather is never a factor when I decide to walk. However, I make exceptions for blizzards and tropical storms. Do you think you'd like to hang out with me?"

"It sounds interesting."

"It's interesting, educational and enlightening. I find myself talking to people I would've ignored if I didn't have a camera. One time I asked a homeless man if I could shoot him, and he said I could if I paid for him to eat."

"Did you?"

Nayo nodded, smiling. "He was very patient when I snapped several candid shots, then we went to a nearby coffee shop and I told him to order whatever he wanted. We got a few dirty looks from some of the customers when we walked in. A waitress opened her mouth to tell me she couldn't serve him, but after I put a tongue-lashing on that heifer, she hung her head in shame."

"Why are they always heifers, Nayo?"

"I'd rather call them heifers than bitches. Once we were seated I noticed something about the man for the first time. Although his clothes appeared dirty, he didn't smell dirty. When I mentioned this to him, he finally admitted that he was an actor who was researching a role for a part in an independent film to be shot on location on the Lower East Side. The clothes came from a studio's wardrobe department."

"Did he get the part?"

"He was selected to be in the film, but when the director saw his audition, he was so impressed with his acting that he gave him a bigger role."

"Do you still keep in touch?"

"We e-mail each other several times a year and get together whenever he's on the East Coast. A couple of years ago he went to London and found what he says was his calling when he bought a pub. He and some other actors stage their own productions for the locals and tourists. All I can say is he's very, very happy."

Ivan tried making out the expression on Nayo's face in the muted light. "What about you, Nayo?"

"What *about* me?" she asked.

"Are you happy?"

"I'd rather use the word *content*."

"Could your life be better?"

"How, Ivan? You tell me how it could be better. I'm not homeless or hungry and I have my health. My career is taking off and I have a dream job that pays well and permits me the time I need to indulge in my fantasies."

Pressing his mouth to her scented neck, Ivan breathed, "What do you fantasize about?"

Nayo gasped. "I can't tell you that!"

"I can always put you on my couch for counseling. After a couple of sessions I won't have to ask you about your fantasies, because you'll open up and tell me."

She wrinkled her nose. "You can't have it both ways, darling. Either I'm on your couch or in your bed. It can't be both."

Ivan knew she was right. He wasn't going to risk losing his license because he couldn't resist sleeping with a patient. Once he began sleeping with Nayo he wanted her to be the last woman in his life.

Even before meeting her, he'd tired of dating a different woman every two or three months. What he hadn't been able to fathom from the first time he, Kyle and Duncan began frequenting clubs was why they never had to employ cheesy pickup lines to get a woman's attention. Women came to them like bees to flowers, sometimes offering to indulge in unspeakable acts that left them more shaken than curious.

Ivan didn't think of himself as a prude, yet drew the line when it came too close to what he knew to be deviant. He'd had his share of one-night stands, each one leaving him more unfulfilled than the one before it. After a while he stopped sleeping with women for a period of time, using the respite as a chance for renewal and rediscovery. When he hadn't gone to New York to reconnect with his friends, they drove down to D.C. to see him, because whenever he went into a funk, he neglected to call those closest to him.

A meltdown sent him to his own therapist who, after two sessions, identified the source of his anxiety. Whenever he celebrated a birthday he was reminded that Jared wasn't there to celebrate with him. Some years he didn't know what was worse—not having Jared there for their birthday or recalling with vivid clarity the exact day and time of his twin's death.

"Ivan?"

He blinked. "What?"

"You just zoned out on me."

"What did I say?"

"It's what you *didn't* say. Let's go back to the table."

Smiling, Ivan swung Nayo around and around in an intricate dance step. "I learned that watching *Dancing with the Stars*," he said proudly.

"Showoff."

"Hell, yeah!"

"Excuse me, brother," Kyle said, tapping him on the shoulder, "but I promised myself that I would dance with every beautiful woman here tonight."

Ivan started to protest, but it was too late. Kyle was dancing off with Nayo, leaving him standing in the middle of the dance floor staring at her petite body pressed against his friend's.

Wending his way between swaying couples, he walked over to the bar and ordered a black dog. The moment he asked the bartender for the cocktail he remembered he'd drunk both his and Nayo's the night they went out on their first date, a night that ended with them leaving the party because he hadn't been able to deal with an unfounded jealousy.

What he hadn't known at the time was that he really liked the pretty photographer, liked her without knowing anything more about her except her name and that she took incredible photographs.

Reaching into the pocket of his trousers, he left a bill on the bar, nodding to the startled bartender when he saw the denomination. Lifting his glass in a salute, he walked back to his table.

Kyle smiled down at the woman in his arms. "Ava told me you're going to photograph our wedding."

"Yes," Nayo said. "I can't believe I'm going to the

Caribbean during the coldest month of the year in the Northeast."

"That's why we decided to get married at a tropical location."

"How many are on your guest list?"

"Forty."

"That's a small wedding."

Nayo had been to weddings where there were more than three hundred guests, seeing the bride and groom overwhelmed by having to acknowledge each guest personally.

"Ava and I wanted to limit it to immediate family and close friends. And because we're holding it at a private resort, we booked all the rooms for the week leading up to and including Valentine's Day. If anyone wants to take a free, all-inclusive vacation, then they're welcome to come for the week."

"That is sweet!"

Kyle winked at her. "I'd say it is."

"How many are going to be in the wedding party?"

"Six. Duncan's going to be my best man, and Ivan and Micah Sanborn will be groomsmen. Ava's sister will be her matron of honor, and Tamara and a coworker will be attendants."

Nayo studied the exquisite bones of Kyle Chatham's face. She'd seen African masks with the same slant of eyes and cheekbones. "Ivan told me he's going to be Duncan's best man."

Kyle's eyes narrowed when he met the round-eyed gaze of the woman who'd changed his best friend. "Of all the women Ivan has gone out with, I can honestly say you top the list."

"He's slept with *that* many women?"

"I didn't say he slept with them. And I really don't know how many women Ivan has dated."

"You had to see him with quite a few to make that statement."

"If we were in a court of law, I'd ask the jury to disregard the statement."

Nayo realized Kyle was either sorry he'd broached the subject or was trying to cover up his faux pas. "Consider it stricken from the record," she teased, smiling.

Kyle knew he had to closely monitor what he said to Nayo Goddard. His comparing her to the other women in Ivan's life was meant to be a compliment, not an opportunity to out his brother about what had become a revolving-door dating game. He'd dated his share of women, too, but Ivan had outdistanced him and Duncan before they were twenty-five. Kyle didn't know what it was, but women were drawn to Ivan's brooding face and personality. More than once he'd heard women refer to him as a "tortured soul."

There was no doubt Ivan and Duncan had experienced traumatic losses, but it was Ivan who'd witnessed death and murder firsthand when his twin brother breathed his last in his arms.

The musical selection ended, and Kyle escorted Nayo back to their table. Duncan and Ivan stood up with their approach.

Nayo sat next to Ivan, smiling when he winked at her. "What are you drinking?"

"It's a black dog."

"Why does that sound so familiar?" she crooned. In a motion, too quick for the eye to follow, she reached for the old-fashioned glass and put it to her lips. Those at the table watched with wide eyes as she downed the drink, then touched the corners of her mouth with a napkin.

Ivan couldn't move. "Oh, sh—" He managed to swallow the expletive.

"Damn!" Kyle and Duncan chorused.

Tamara gave Ava a fist bump. "That's what I'm talking about."

Ava flashed a grin. "I told you that little bit could hang."

Kyle stared at Ivan, then Duncan. "It sounds as if the ladies just challenged us to a throw-down."

"No, the ladies didn't," Nayo countered.

"Didn't you say something about hangin'?" Duncan drawled.

Tamara pulled her fiancé's ear. "To us hanging doesn't mean doing shots, darling."

Kyle cut his eyes at his two friends. "I'm glad you clarified that, because anytime you ladies want a throw-down, we'll oblige."

"Speak for yourself, brother," Ivan said, deadpan. "I learned a long time ago that females are more competitive than their male counterparts, and it usually ends up with them winning or a no-contest."

Kyle and Duncan exchanged a look, then threw their napkins at Ivan, who'd dissolved into a paroxysm of laughter that had other guests staring at their table. Their antics set the stage for a frivolity that lasted until Simone and Rafe cut their cake and the waitstaff distributed pieces of it as souvenirs.

A hush descended on the ballroom when Simone walked over to Nayo and handed her the bridal bouquet. Kyle and Duncan crossed their arms over their chests as if they'd rehearsed the gesture and stared at a stunned Ivan.

"Are you holding out on us, Campbell?"

Ivan stared at Nayo as she glared at him. "No."

The tense moment passed when Nayo excused herself, picked up her evening bag and went to the restroom. There, she sat on a cushioned bench in the lounge area, trying to fathom exactly what had gone on in the ballroom.

Why had Simone given her the bouquet when the tradition was to throw it to the single women and the one to catch it would be the next one to marry? Looping one leg over the other, her shoe-clad foot beat a tattoo on the marble floor.

The door opened and she glanced up to find Tamara

staring at her. "I'm all right," she said before the doctor could say anything.

"May I sit?" Tamara asked.

"Sure." She moved over and Tamara sat beside her.

Reaching for Nayo's hand, Tamara held it, surreptitiously taking her pulse. "You love him, don't you?"

Nayo stared at the statuesque woman with the gorgeous face. Tonight Tamara wore her hair in a mass of tiny curls that floated above her bared shoulders. There was no doubt Tamara and Duncan would produce beautiful children.

"Is it that obvious?"

"Maybe not to Ivan, but it is to me and Ava."

"Damn, I didn't think I was that transparent."

"You're no more transparent than Ivan."

"What are you talking about?"

"Your boyfriend has a real bad case of the love jones."

Nayo sat up straighter. "How do you know this?"

"To say I'm nosy is an understatement," Tamara admitted, smiling. "I stayed over at Duncan's place one night last week and I heard him on the phone with Kyle. He thought I was asleep when he activated the speaker feature on his phone because he was going through his closet looking for a particular jacket. They were talking about Ivan, about how he's changed since he started seeing you. Kyle said that he'd asked Ivan how he felt about you, and the L-word came up. Then

Duncan said something about Ivan's going to be the next one to pop the question. And of course I took that to mean that he's going to ask you to marry him."

Nayo closed her eyes as she felt the hot sting of tears behind her eyelids. "Even if he does ask me, I can't accept."

"Why not, Nayo? You're in love with the man. I don't mind admitting that if I'd met Ivan first, I would've been all over him. He's brilliant, gorgeous and he passed the test."

Nayo opened her eyes. "What test?"

"When you asked him to go to the supermarket in the middle of a football game, he didn't hesitate. Duncan's a pussycat, but if I'd had asked to go he would've turned on me like a rogue lion. He's never let me forget I asked him to buy a home pregnancy test for Tessa the day we hosted a party to celebrate Ava and Kyle's engagement. Kyle and Ivan still tease him about it."

"Ivan's very accommodating."

"That's because Ivan is in love with you, Nayo. I was married before, so I'm familiar with dogs masquerading as men. I work in a male-dominated profession, which means I've dealt with the good ones, the not-so-good ones and a few I would like to shave with a scalpel. A word of advice—act tardy, and some other woman will come along and scoop up your man."

"He's never said that he loves me."

"Men are slow like that, Nayo. They'll usually blurt out all kinds of stuff when they're ejaculating. Close your mouth, girl, because I'm sure you've heard it."

Nayo nodded in agreement. Ivan had told her he loves the way she makes him feel whenever he's inside her; he loves her smell; he loves her face, body, but he has yet to say he loves *her*.

"When I got involved with Ivan it wasn't to get a husband, Tamara."

"Were you ever married?"

"No."

"Engaged?"

"Once," Nayo admitted. "I ended it because I found out he was using me."

Tamara twisted her lush mouth. "I belonged to the same club. Don't you want to marry?"

"Yes, but not now."

A beat passed as Tamara gave the photographer a pointed look. "What's stopping you, Nayo?"

"My career. I'm not where I want to be in my career."

"And neither am I, but I'm not going to let that stop me from grasping a little happiness before I die. Duncan had planned to marry the weekend following the World Trade Center disaster, but it never happened because his fiancée was one of the thousands who lost their lives that day. I worked for thirty-six hours without sleep and I always wonder if he was one of the people who came to the hospital looking for word of their loved ones.

When those people got up that morning, they never envisioned not coming home.

"Come June I plan to marry Duncan Gilmore and hopefully get pregnant on my wedding night. Our marriage is not going to be easy, because I'll be working nights and Duncan days. But whenever we're together, I'm going to make certain it's quality time."

"Are you going give up practicing medicine?"

"I'll probably take a leave for a couple of years to bond with my baby. And, if I decide not to return to the hospital, I can always set up a practice or go in with another doctor. There are solutions to every problem. Meanwhile, you have an advantage over Ava and me because you freelance. You can select where and when you want to accept a commission. I had to submit a request to take a week off in February for Ava's wedding, and then I had to wait for my supervisor to approve it. All you have to do is pack your clothes and equipment and you're done."

"I do have a job."

"Where and doing what?" Nayo told her about her position with the auction house. "Please, Nayo. You work part-time, and with today's economy not too many people are buying big-ticket items. Even if you decide to give up your part-time gig, you still have your photography to fall back on. Tessa told me she's going to use you as a Signature Bridals photographer, and you know what that means."

"Big-time exposure."

"There you go," Tamara drawled. "Now, are you ready to go back to your man? Take it from someone who knows—you leave your man alone too long and some heifer will move in and try to lure him away."

Nayo laughed because Tamara said "heifer," which had become her favorite word for women of an unsavory nature. She stood up and smoothed the front of her dress. Then she hugged Tamara.

"Thanks for the pep talk."

Tamara, bending slightly, returned the hug. "Anytime, girlfriend."

"Give me a minute to touch up my lips, then I'll be ready."

When Nayo walked out of the lounge with Tamara, she was ready for Ivan and whatever the future held for them.

Chapter 17

Ivan draped his coat and suit jacket over the back of the dining-area chair before he folded his tall frame down onto the tufted yellow sofa in Nayo's living room. There were advantages and disadvantages to living in a studio apartment, and watching Nayo undress was definitely an advantage.

He stared, unable to move or speak as she unzipped her dress and stepped out of it. The flesh between his legs stirred to life. Ivan felt like a voyeur when he couldn't pull his gaze away from her half-nude body. Erotic fantasies came to life when he stared at her legs encased in sheer navy nylons attached to a lacy garter belt and her tiny feet in the matching stilettos. Her firm breasts swayed gently when she bent down to slip off her heels.

Ivan swallowed a groan as he tried not to squirm on the sofa. Watching Nayo undress was akin to watching burlesque, where the dancer teased and tantalized. He must have groaned again, because she turned to look at him.

"Are you all right?"

"No."

Nayo set aside her shoes. "What's the matter?"

He closed his eyes. "I'm in pain, baby."

Nayo rushed over to the sofa, her heart beating double-time. Ivan had clutched his chest. "Oh, no!" she cried. Was he having a heart attack? "Ivan! Ivan, talk to me."

Ivan heard the panic in her voice and opened his eyes. "Yes, doll face."

"Where's the pain?"

His hand moved lower, resting over his belt buckle. "It's here."

Scrambling onto the sofa, she placed her hand over his. "Show me where it is."

"It's moving around."

"Where!" Nayo was practically screaming.

"Take off my belt." It was becoming more difficult for Ivan to keep up the ruse, because he couldn't control his growing erection.

Nayo hadn't realized her hands were shaking uncontrollably until she attempted to undo the button on his waistband. She unzipped the fly and slipped her hand through the opening. She couldn't remember if the appendix was on the right or the left. Where was Tamara when she needed her?

"Show me where it hurts, darling."

Ivan took her hand and guided it to his penis. It took her several seconds to realize he'd played a trick on her. "I'm sorry, baby," he said when she narrowed her eyes at him.

"You're sorry, Ivan Campbell! I thought you were having a heart attack."

He pointed to his chest. "I didn't say the pain was here."

"Oh, no?"

She drew back her fist to hit him, but Ivan's reflexes were too fast. Holding her wrist in a firm grip, he eased her onto her back, covering her mouth with his and stopping her protests.

"Don't fight me, baby," he said against her parted lips.

"Why not? What you just did is cruel, Ivan."

He smiled. "You think so," he whispered.

Nayo stopped struggling, because she knew she was no match for his superior strength. He released her wrist. "Yes."

Ivan gazed at the face of the woman he loved beyond description. "I am in pain, Nayo, because I love you." He ignored her gasp. "You came into my life at the time of the year when, if I had the power, I'd blot it off the calendar. Whenever the days grow shorter, the color of the leaves change and fall to the ground, I feel as if I'm dying."

Going to her knees, Nayo wrapped her arms around Ivan's head and pressed his face to her naked breasts. "You're alive, darling."

"I am when I'm with you."

She rested her chin on the top of his head. "You're alive when we're not together, too. Even when we're apart I still can feel you, smell you and fantasize about making love with you."

"You don't understand. You can't understand."

Nayo pulled back, cradling Ivan's face between her hands. With wide eyes, she saw the pain in his. "Come to bed."

"I need to tell you something."

"Tell me in bed."

She moved off the sofa and he got up with her. Hand in hand, they walked to the bed. Nayo took over. She undressed Ivan, covering his magnificent naked body with a sheet and lightweight blanket. She finished undressing herself, turned off the lamp and got in to straddle his body.

"Talk to me, darling."

She listened, her heart keeping tempo with his as Ivan talked about being an identical twin. "Although Jared and I looked exactly alike, we were nothing alike. He was outgoing and made friends easily, while I was content to hang out with Kyle and DG. Jared met a girl who lived in East Harlem and he used to sneak out to meet her."

"How old was he?"

"Thirteen. My father warned him about leaving the neighborhood, but Jared's hormones were raging. I didn't find out until much later that the girl wasn't thirteen, as he told me, but seventeen."

Nayo closed her eyes, knowing what Ivan was going to say. "Were they sleeping together?"

"Yeah. One night he came home with a busted lip, and when I asked him what happened, he claimed he tripped and fell. But I knew differently, Nayo. When you're a twin you feel things a person who's single birth can't feel. Whenever Jared disappeared I knew he was sneaking off to see that girl. I tried to tell him she's was just using him, but he didn't believe it. He said I would change my opinion once I met her.

"It was a rainy Saturday in October when Jared told me that he'd made arrangements for me to meet his girl-friend. We walked to a housing project on the east side, sat down on a bench and waited. Jared stood up when a girl came out of one of the buildings, and we followed her to the corner. I supposed she and Jared had some sort of ritual, that he wouldn't say anything to her until they were a certain distance away from the housing project. She crossed the street, but instead of following, Jared waited for another light to change.

"While we were standing there a car pulled up and

someone sitting in the passenger-side seat pointed a gun at us. He got off two rounds, hitting Jared in the chest, before they sped off. I sat on the sidewalk in the rain watching my brother die in my arms. When the police and ambulance arrived his face was covered with leaves from an overhead tree.

"I spent years blaming myself for my brother's death, because instead of going with him to meet some girl who was on some power trip because she could lead a thirteen-year-old boy around by his gonads, I should've told my parents what he was doing and where he was going."

"You tried to warn him, Ivan, but he wouldn't listen."

"I didn't do enough, Nayo."

"I know it doesn't minimize the loss and pain, but that day your parents could've lost two sons, instead of one. Didn't you say you and Jared were identical?"

"Yeah, but we never dressed alike. When they pulled up they knew which twin to shoot."

"Do you think the girl set up your brother to be shot?"

"I don't know. I'll never know because I didn't get a good look at her face. And when the police went around the projects asking questions, everyone became deaf, blind and mute. They knew nothing. They saw nothing. They heard nothing. It took my mother a long time to accept losing a child. My looking exactly like Jared didn't make it any easier."

"Is losing your brother the reason why you fear commitment? You're afraid of loving and losing?"

"Yes."

"Are you afraid of losing me, Ivan?"

"I don't know."

"You said you love me. Well, I love you, too, Ivan, and I'm not afraid of losing you."

He smiled. "You're a lot more confident than I am, because you know I'm not going anywhere."

"Neither am I."

"Prove it to me, baby."

Nayo shifted into a more comfortable position, her legs sandwiched between his hair-roughened ones. "What do you want me to do?"

"Marry me, Nayo Goddard."

The seconds ticked off as Nayo recalled her conversation with Tamara earlier that evening. She thought about Duncan losing his fiancée and Ivan cradling his dead brother in his arms.

"I marry you, Ivan Campbell, and what?"

"What do you mean, what?"

"What do I do?"

"You move in with me. And if you want I'll turn the top floor into a gallery for you. I suppose that means I'll have to put in an elevator, but it will be worth it when people from the art world come to see my wife's brilliant photographs. Working from home will give you all the time you need to balance your career and motherhood."

Her head came up. "You want children?"

Ivan smiled. "As many as you're willing to give me. Will you marry me, Nayo?"

"I think so."

"Is that a yes or a no?"

"It's a yes."

Everything was happening so quickly that Nayo couldn't sort it out. Ivan didn't give her a chance to catch her breath when he reversed their positions and eased his sex into her body. Feeling his hardness inside her without the layer of latex stole the breath from her lungs. Within minutes the first spasm of pleasure ripped through her.

She was on fire!

Her breath was coming in deep sobs, escalating with each strong thrust of Ivan's hips. Tamara had mentioned men blurting out things in the throes of passion, but it was she who urged Ivan on.

"Harder, baby. Deeper! That's it," she chanted over and over until it became a litany.

Ivan knew this coming together was different, not only because it was the first time since he'd become sexually active that he hadn't used protection, but because he knew the woman writhing under him would be the last woman in his life.

Nayo's attempt to prolong climaxing proved futile. She loved him, loved him more than any man she'd ever known. She'd fought Ivan and fought her feelings, but realized that in the greater scheme of things, life was short, tomorrow wasn't promised, and she was going to seize the happiness offered her. The spasms became stronger and stronger until the dam broke, and she sobbed Ivan's name as she was hurtled beyond reality.

Ivan felt the heat of Nayo's breath, the sound of her calling his name in his ear as he released his passion inside her warm, moist body, chanting, "I love you, I love you," the admission torn from his throat and heart. At last he collapsed, sated, on her moist body.

"Ivan."

"Yes, doll face."

"I don't think we should wait too long to set a wedding date."

"Why?"

Nayo smiled when she fantasized her body swollen with Ivan's child. "You picked the wrong time of the month to make love to me without protection."

Ivan nuzzled her neck. "No, I didn't. It just means we have to set an early wedding date."

"How early?"

"How's Beaver Run during Christmas?"

"Cold and very festive."

Ivan cradled Nayo to his body as he reversed their positions. "Call and tell your mother to expect her future son-in-law this coming weekend. I know we're not giving her much time, but I'm willing to pay Tessa whatever she wants to make you a Signature bride."

Nayo curved her body into Ivan's. She'd known

there was something special about Ivan when he walked
into Magnus Galleries to view her exhibition. What she
hadn't known at the time was that he would become her
lover, husband and hopefully the father of her children.

Epilogue

Nayo had always wanted to be a June bride; if not June, then a summer bride. However, nothing could have prepared her for the ethereal setting unfolding before her eyes when her father escorted her through the door of the darkened church illuminated only by candlelight. After the ceremony, guests would file through a hallway into a heated barn for a buffet dinner and a night of dancing.

She'd returned to Beaver Run the week before to prepare for her wedding to Ivan Garner Campbell. His parents, sister, brother-in-law and niece arrived Christmas Eve in time to share dinner with the Goddards. Her father had outdone himself when he prepared a Christmas dinner fit for a king, while her mother insisted the Campbells stay at their farmhouse, rather than a nearby motel.

Signature Bridals had come through when wedding planner Tessa traveled to Beaver Run to survey the location for the winter wedding and reception. Her rounded face and expanding waistline were obvious indicators that she was with child.

Tessa sent out invitations, while Simone Whitfield-Madison ordered flowers for the church and barn where the reception would be held. Faith McMillan, because of her impending due date, discussed the design of the wedding cake and filling to Nayo by phone.

Ivan had the last laugh when he teased Kyle and Duncan about beating them to the altar, but they took it in stride, because in another six months all the best men would be married men. Ivan couldn't decide if he wanted Kyle or Duncan as his best man, so he broke tradition and chose both.

The last chords of Beethoven's Ninth Symphony faded and the string quartet of two violins, a viola and cello played the familiar strains of the Wedding March. Nayo was certain her father felt her trembling as they progressed down the aisle to the front of a church filled with friends, family and curious onlookers from Beaver Run who'd come to witness one of their own marry someone from downstate.

A ripple of shock went through those in the assembly who didn't recognize Steven Goddard without his white bibbed apron. His chest seemed to swell as he escorted his daughter to the man waiting to make her his wife.

"Who gives this woman in marriage?" asked the minister in a deep, sonorous voice that floated throughout the rustic church.

Steven Goddard took a breath and smiled at his daughter. "I do." Leaning over, he kissed Nayo before placing her hand on Ivan's outstretched one. He stepped back and sat in the pew next to his wife. They shared a smile, then a kiss before settling back to watch the exchange of vows between their daughter and the man who'd promised to love and protect Nayo for the rest of his life.

Nayo smiled at Ivan as he tightened his hold on her hand and mouthed, "I love you."

"Me, too," she mouthed back.

Peter Demetrious captured the unabashed love in the bride's eyes. He'd come to Beaver Run to photograph the Goddard-Campbell nuptials because Tessa Whitfield-Sanborn told him she'd finally met a photographer who was not only a woman but his equal.

Peter said if he found truth in her pronouncement, he wouldn't charge for photographing the wedding. He'd left L.A. and its seventy-degree temperature to fly to Beaver Run, where he'd encountered below-freezing temperatures, on a challenge.

Much to his chagrin he was photographing the wedding—for free!

The exchange of rings, their first kiss as husband and wife and a shared smile were captured for perpetuity.